Murder Is Chartered

A Susan Wiles Schoolhouse Mystery

by

Diane Weiner

Copyright 2017 by Diane Weiner

For information, email **Cozy Cat Press**, cozycatpress@aol.com or visit our website at: www.cozycatpress.com

COZY CAT
PRESS

ISBN: 978-1-946063-12-0

Printed in the United States of America

Cover design by Paula Ellenberger
www.paulaellenberger.com

1 2 3 4 5 6 7 8 9 10

This book is dedicated to foster and adoptive parents everywhere for opening their hearts and making a difference in a child's life.

Chapter 1

Stifling a yawn, Susan pumped up the volume on the radio of her Prius. The black, starless, rural New York sky contributed to her desire to curl up in her bed after the marathon day she'd had. It was her own fault. Her drive to feel productive in her retirement led to spending many days back in school—only now she wasn't getting paid for it.

Currently, she was volunteering in her friend Theresa's fourth grade classroom at the new charter school. Tonight was Westbrook Charter's inaugural open house. She'd offered to help set up, but wound up staying through a presentation that extended long past the scheduled ending time. All those parents pumping Theresa for information about their children—children Theresa still barely knew after only a few weeks of school.

I should have run out for dinner rather than loading up on the cookies and punch the school offered. She fought with her body to stay awake for another fifteen minutes. By then she'd be home with Mike and her cats.

Susan squinted to minimize the glare on her windshield as she followed the twisty road through the mountains. The streetlights became farther and farther apart as Westbrook Charter School disappeared from her rearview mirror. By day, the trees donned their spectacular fall attire, but in the dark, she felt as though she was driving through Sleepy Hollow with the headless horseman on her tail.

Her mind wandered to her recent visit with her friends in Vermont—much more relaxing than the first visit she and Mike had made back in February, where flashes of embarrassing snowshoe spills and the image of the dead body they'd discovered in her friend Emily's office made her shudder. She yawned audibly. *Stay awake, Susan. You're almost home.*

Then she thought about her new granddaughter, Mia, whom Lynette and Jason had brought home from China last spring. She glowed thinking about Mia and her first granddaughter, Annalise. *I can't wait to cook with Annalise and try making the lo mein recipe I learned in my Chinese cooking class. At four years old, surely she can stir the noodles with the sauce or sprinkle chopped scallions on top.* Her head throbbed, and her stomach growled.

Her phone vibrated on the passenger seat. *Audrey. I'm not going to answer it. I don't feel like hearing about her happy new marriage to her ex-con boyfriend. At least now George and I won't have to tend to our mother after she lands in a nursing home. We'll leave that up to Richard.* The thought didn't really appease her. At eighty, Audrey still finished the *New York Times* crossword puzzle in record time. At the rate she was going, she'd be living on her own into her hundreds.

Her head felt as heavy as a sack of rocks, and her eyes were surrendering. *Stay awake, Susan.* She reached into her purse for a pack of almonds. Then she remembered the candy bar in her tote bag and opted for it instead. Protein took a while to be absorbed, but sugar—that was immediate energy.

She slammed on the brakes when she heard a thump smacking down on the hood of her car. She froze.

Oh my God! Did I hit someone? I only looked away for a second. Through a cracked windshield, she peered in front of her but couldn't tell. She grabbed the door handle with her sweaty hand. *Did I fall asleep at the wheel?* The last thing she remembered was reaching for the candy bar, but she felt foggy and couldn't be sure she hadn't dozed off.

She ran out of the car, shivering when the night air hit her perspiration-soaked body. She ran her finger over the hood, then gingerly peeked at the road in front of her bumper, illuminated by the headlights. She felt like she was going to throw up. A mangled body in a tweed coat was sprawled in front of the car. Trembling, she touched her fingers to the woman's neck, feeling for a nonexistent pulse. *My God, did I just kill this woman?* Grabbing her cell phone from the car, she turned off the ignition and called her detective daughter.

"Lynette. I... I need your help. There's a body. I think I hit her. I can't find a pulse."

"A body? Mom, calm down. Where are you? Are you in your car? It's probably a deer. Did you call 911?"

Susan looked around, then up at the rusty railroad bridge she'd been about to drive under, answering the questions in the order in which they were asked. "I... I'm just in front of the railroad bridge... on Waffle Hollow Road. Not yet. I'm sure she's... she isn't moving. Her body's all twisted. I'm sure she's... she's..."

"Mom, I'll call 911, and I'll be right there. Hang on."

I must have fallen asleep at the wheel and hit her. I killed someone. She heaved vomit onto the road. Shaking, she wiped her mouth on the sleeve of her cardigan and, careful not to move anything, bent down to see the woman's face. *Oh no! I know her. I can't believe I just killed her. I killed her!*

She imagined the police telling the victim's husband his wife was hit by a car and didn't survive. She imagined telling Mike what she'd done. She pictured a trial... the jury saying *guilty*... being locked in a jail cell. She'd visited jails before. She'd rather die than spend her life there. *What if I get the death penalty? God, I didn't mean the part I said about rather being dead.*

She collapsed on the ground, feeling alone, ashamed, afraid. Racked with guilt, she hugged her knees and waited for the police. After what felt like an eternity, she heard sirens and worked her way to a standing position. Lynette, blond ponytail swishing behind her, ran out of her car, followed by a cruiser and an ambulance. The EMTs went directly to the body. Lynette went directly to her mother and hugged her.

"Mom, are you okay? What happened?"

"I was driving home from open house. I felt dizzy and may have fallen asleep at the wheel." Lynette closed her mouth tightly. Susan knew she was holding her tongue. "I heard a loud crash on the car. I thought maybe I'd hit a deer. Then I got out, went to the front of the car, and saw her. I prayed she was alive, but I felt for a pulse and knew she wasn't." Sobs rolled out of her mouth and eyes.

"Mom, it was an accident. Don't say anything about falling asleep at the wheel. You said you thought you did, but you weren't sure."

"But."

"Listen to me, or things will be worse. It was dark. Who walks out in the dark on a night like this on a lonely mountain road? Maybe she meant to get hit. Suicide by car. I'll see if there was an insurance policy. They pay out for accidents but not suicide..."

"Lynette! It was my fault."

"Don't say anything without a lawyer here. I've got your statement. Let's go to the hospital and be sure you're okay. And we'll get a blood test to prove you weren't drinking or on drugs."

"But Lynette. It wasn't suicide. I know her. She was at the open house. It's the assistant principal, Melissa Chadwick. She was smiling and greeting parents just an hour or two ago."

Lynette's partner, Jackson Simpson, approached. "Lynette, Susan, what's going on?" He put his hand on Susan's shoulder. "Are you okay? Do you need a doctor?"

Lynette said, "There was an accident. Can you stay and wait for the medical examiner?"

Susan wobbled and fell to the ground.

"Mom! Jackson, help me get her up." They each put a supporting arm around Susan's waist. Let's get her to my car."

The headlights from the cruiser stung her eyes. Susan mumbled, "I'm okay. I just got a little dizzy."

A rookie officer came over. "Detective Green, want me to take a statement?"

"No," said Lynette, "go make sure you get photos from all angles, and mark any evidence so we can determine what happened here. We're going to the hospital. You've got this? Right, Jackson?"

"Of course." He waited for the officer to get out of earshot. "Susan, weren't you at the open house with Theresa?" Theresa was Jackson's wife and mother of their ten-month-old baby boy.

"Yes. She should be home by now."

"Lynette, call me as soon as you know your mom's okay. I'll take care of this. Did you hit the victim, Susan?"

"Not just a victim," said Lynette. "It's the assistant

principal from the charter school. Theresa's boss. Looks like she ran out into the road. Mom couldn't stop in time."

Susan opened her mouth to speak, but Lynette squeezed her arm, nearly breaking her skin with her nails. Lynette waved Jackson on.

"Go ahead and make sure the scene is handled correctly."

Susan felt like a lobster about to be dropped into boiling water. Lynette was always black and white about the law. The fact that she stifled her when she tried to talk to Jackson and how she was rushing her away to the hospital meant this was serious. Not that Susan hadn't already come to that conclusion. *I can't let Lynette cover for me. She'll lose her job.*

"Lynette, take me down to the station. This was all my fault."

"This doesn't look right. I've seen my share of hit-and-runs in my career, and the positioning is all wrong. It makes no sense that she was out here at this hour. Keep your guilt to yourself until we investigate and know exactly what happened."

Chapter 2

Susan's head throbbed. All she wanted was to go back home and curl up in her bed, but Lynette insisted on taking her to the hospital. She leaned her head against the passenger side window, wishing the night had never happened. Soon the hospital lights flooded through the car window.

"Come on, Mom. Dad's meeting us here."

Lynette led Susan into the emergency room, full of sick zombies waiting in hard plastic chairs. Susan held her breath to avoid the stench of fast food and sweat. The only time she enjoyed being in a hospital was when she was visiting a newborn. Her mind flashed to the night Annalise was born.

"Is this really necessary, Lynette? Since when do I drink anything stronger than coffee? And I assure you there are no drugs in my system."

"Of course not, but we have to protect you. This way we have solid proof that you weren't under the influence in case the victim's family tries to sue. And you know they will. Besides, you passed out at the scene. Something's not right."

Or if I have to prove in court I wasn't under the influence. She didn't want to go there. "I'm just tired and hungry."

Susan couldn't stop thinking about the sound of the woman hitting the hood of her Prius. By now, Melissa Chadwick's husband would have been notified of her death. What if the police came tonight to arrest her? She was still wearing work clothes and hadn't brushed her teeth after the punch and cookies at the open house. She briefly considered asking Mike to bring sweats and a toothbrush to the hospital just in case. Too late.

"Susan, are you okay? What happened?" Mike appeared and wrapped his arms around her. The lingering scent of Irish Spring shampoo in his wavy, dark hair and the stubble of his five-o'clock shadow were comforting.

"I'm shaky and sick to my stomach. I killed her, Mike. I'll never forgive myself."

"Mom," said Lynette, "first of all, don't go saying you killed her. We don't know for sure that's the case."

"I'm quite sure she was dead. There was no pulse when I checked, and I saw the EMTs cover her face with a sheet as we were leaving."

"She is dead, but we still don't know why she was out in the middle of the road like that. I don't think it's what it looks like."

A middle-aged nurse with honey-colored skin and a reassuring manner led them through double doors and into a cubicle. She took a brief history, drew blood, and remarked on Susan's high blood pressure. *After what I went through tonight, of course my blood pressure is high.*

"I'll get this to the lab, and the doctor will be in shortly." The nurse pulled the curtain shut behind her.

Susan turned to her daughter. "Can I go home, or am I being arrested?"

"Calm down. Do you want me to run down to the cafeteria and get you some food while we wait? It's long past dinnertime. There's a McDonald's in the lobby. I can see if it's open."

Susan's stomach growled. Until Lynette mentioned it, she'd forgotten how hungry she was. Even under the most severe of stresses, she had never been one of those people who lost their appetite. In fact, stress made her want to eat more. She nodded to Lynette.

"Okay, maybe a sandwich and a Diet Coke."

Lynette pulled the curtain behind her. Mike sat in the metal chair next to the bed.

"Susan, you were driving home from the open house. Melissa Chadwick was there too, correct? What was she doing in your path? Did she just dart out from nowhere?"

"I don't know. I saw her earlier in the evening when the parents gathered in the cafeteria before heading to the classrooms. I didn't see her after that until... I turned away for a moment to reach into my bag. I don't know if I dozed off. I was exhausted and hungry. I heard the body hit the hood. No. Wait. I heard her hit the roof of the car. Then there was another impact. I think she hit the top of the car and then the hood. Oh, I'm so mixed up. First I thought I'd hit an animal."

Mike squeezed her hand. "It's going to be okay. You certainly didn't do it on purpose. The road was dark, right? The streetlights are pretty sparse along that stretch." He hugged her silently, always her safe harbor. She closed her eyes and held on tightly. The curtain snapped open, startling her.

A young doctor with a stethoscope around his neck stared down at a clipboard. "How are you feeling, ma'am?"

"I'm fine. I just want to go home and go to bed."

"We rushed the blood work, and there are no traces of alcohol or drugs in your system."

"I could have told you that," said Susan.

Lynette came in with a plastic-wrapped sandwich and a can of soda. "The cafeteria was closed, but I found a vending machine." She introduced herself to the doctor. "I heard you say the blood work was clean."

"Clean as far as drugs or alcohol. The blood sugar, however, was high. Especially since she hadn't eaten in several hours."

"What does that mean?" asked Mike.

"She should make an appointment ASAP with her regular doctor to rule out diabetes."

In unison, Mike, Lynette, and Susan said, "Diabetes?"

Susan's night couldn't get much worse. First she believed she was probably going to jail, and now she may be diabetic. She had been slacking on her walks and yoga classes lately, but in spite of it, she'd lost a few pounds.

"Have you been extra thirsty lately? Headaches?"

"Now that you mention it…"

"Let's not jump the gun. With a few healthy lifestyle changes, you'll hopefully be able to get your blood sugar under control without medication."

"Medication? You mean insulin?"

"First things first. Go home and get some rest."

After the doctor left, Lynette said, "Mom, maybe the diabetes caused you to get confused or pass out."

"Whoa. He said I *may* have diabetes. Don't go getting ahead of ourselves."

"You have to call your doctor first thing in the morning. Meanwhile, go home. I'll get in touch with Jackson and see if they know anything after studying the accident scene. I'll call you in the morning."

When she got home, Susan crawled right into bed. She fell asleep immediately, then woke up a few hours later, unable to turn off her mind. Ludwig and Johann were asleep on either side of her, purring as she stroked them. She noted how restlessly Mike slept beside her. She could skip volunteering today, but Mike was due at the city permit's office bright and early. Another thing to feel guilty about—sending her exhausted husband to work because of her carelessness. She rolled over, trying to think of any lawyers she knew. When she couldn't come up with any, she ran through a list of her friends and acquaintances who she thought might know a defense attorney.

She must have fallen back asleep because she was jolted awake by the sound of her phone. She could hear Mike in the shower.

"Lynette? Did you find out anything? Am I going to jail? Can I get bail at least while I'm awaiting trial?"

"Mom, stop it. I have some good news. I was up half the night talking to Jackson and poring over the accident scene. You didn't kill Melissa Chadwick."

"Of course I did. I saw her body on the street, dead in front of my car."

"She was already dead when you hit her. She fell from the railroad bridge."

"The railroad bridge? What was she doing up there? Did she jump?"

"No. The fall didn't kill her either. Looks like she was strangled. She didn't die there. Her body was dragged onto the bridge and thrown over the railing."

"That's great news. Wait. I mean, it's awful that she's dead, but I didn't kill her, right?"

"Right, Mom. You didn't kill her, but someone did. We're looking at murder."

Chapter 3

Susan told Mike the good news as she passed him exiting the shower. *How can I actually feel happy that a woman is dead?* She stepped into the shower and felt a bushel of worries fall off her shoulders and wash down the drain with the spray of water that soothed her aching body. Now she could focus and help Lynette figure out who killed Melissa Chadwick. She dried off with a freshly washed towel, drinking in the lingering, lavender aroma from the laundry detergent.

"Susan," Mike called from the bedroom, "I'm going now. Call me after you talk to Lynette. And don't go getting in the middle of this. I know how tempting murders are to you. Leave it to the police—promise?"

She sighed entering the bedroom, fingers crossed behind her back. "I promise."

"And remember to call your doctor." Mike headed out.

Remember to call my doctor. Yeah, yeah. She threw on black stretch pants and an oversized blue sweater that matched her eyes. She wiped off her bifocals, dried her hair, and went downstairs to the kitchen where she poured Meow Mix into the cat food bowls.

As she ate her steel-cut oatmeal, she dreaded the conversation she'd inevitably have with her doctor, who was barely older than her own son. It would start with him chastising her for not losing those twenty pounds, and would segue into a prescription to exercise and him scribbling down the phone number for Weight Watchers. It was too early to call his office, and she really had to get down to the station. She'd make an appointment later—if she remembered.

At her detective daughter's request, an officer had driven Susan's Prius back to her house the previous night. When she got to the station, Lynette motioned Susan into her office. Jackson, eating a chocolate donut that was perched on his paunch, was seated next to the desk.

"Want one? There's a whole box in the break room."

She really did want one but not with Lynette watching her. *Five, four, three.*

"Mom, did you call your doctor?"

"Too early. I'll call as soon as I get home. Now about this murder…"

Lynette shuffled papers while Jackson grabbed a legal pad off her desk.

"Mom, what do you know about Melissa Chadwick?"

"I've only worked with her a few months since the new charter school opened and Theresa asked me to volunteer. She's married—was married—to Matthew Chadwick, the CEO of Agrowmex. You know, that company that moved into town and funded the charter school so its employees could secure *a top-notch education* for their children. Frankly, I don't see what's wrong with Westbrook Elementary. A detective and a soon-to-be doctor—you and Evan—got your education in a public school and both of you turned out fine."

"Okay, Mom, I know how most of the town felt about the charter school opening, and I'm all for public education, but stay focused."

"First a factory farming plant, then a charter school. And the CEO makes his wife the assistant principal when there were plenty of homegrown, qualified candidates. That riled a few tempers. Maybe that was the motive." She eyed the last piece of donut as her daughter's partner popped it into his mouth.

Jackson brushed the crumbs off his lap. "Theresa says the assistant principal over at Westbrook Elementary was pretty angry when he was passed over. He's had over a decade of experience and was hoping for the bigger salary the charter school pays."

"Larry Frisina. That's true," said Susan. "Melissa Chadwick had zero experience. She'd never even taught."

"Nepotism's a way of life," said Jackson, shrugging his shoulders.

Susan continued: "And there's that outspoken music teacher over at Westbrook. Duncan Sitwell. He's been hollering since Agrowmex broke ground about letting a Mexican company come in and take American jobs. Ridiculous. The Chadwicks are native New Yorkers. They went down to Mexico to open the company years ago, and now they're moving it back here. Most of the workers are Americans, and those that aren't have legitimate visas."

Lynette said, "Do you remember the protests when the plant first opened? And the periodic vandalism we're still seeing?"

"Yeah," said Jackson. "That hippie group outside of town led by that Hops woman kicked and screamed about factory farming coming to our town. Ah, Della Hops, leader of the commune—I mean co-op. Didn't we arrest her?"

"We did. She tried to attack Matthew Chadwick in his driveway. Threw eggs at him. Organic eggs."

Distracted by her grumbling stomach, Susan wished she'd eaten a heartier breakfast. "So that's three possible suspects so far. First Duncan Sitwell, openly anti-Mexican band teacher at Westbrook Elementary. He's had a grudge against Agrowmex and the Chadwicks ever since he was slammed with a double whammy. He's against foreigners, and he was bullied into selling his family home because Agrowmex needed the land."

Susan found it ironic. Duncan Sitwell taught elementary band at Westbrook Elementary but was making some nice extra income giving music lessons after school to the charter school students, many of whom were Hispanic. *Hypocrite.*

Lynette said, "Then there's the assistant principal at Westbrook Elementary, Larry Frisina. He felt entitled to Melissa's job."

"And last, but not least, Della Hops and her band of hippies," added Jackson.

Susan wondered if Matthew Chadwick himself had been questioned. She'd seen enough *Dateline* episodes to know to suspect the spouse. The Chadwicks appeared to be the happiest of couples. Then again, so did Angelina Jolie and Brad Pitt.

"Have you questioned Matthew Chadwick?"

Lynette answered, "He's flying in this morning. He was on a business trip in Mexico City." She looked at the time on her phone. "As a matter of fact, he should be here any minute."

Susan lingered, hoping to be present when Matthew Chadwick arrived. Even though she hadn't caused his wife's death, having Melissa's dead body land on her Prius somehow had bonded them, and she already felt involved. She'd previously proven herself valuable in the mystery-solving department.

"Mom, go on home. I'll call you later. Make that doctor appointment."

Susan slowly retrieved her sweater from the chair and inched toward the door. Meanwhile, Lynette's phone rang on her desk.

"He's here. Bye, Mom."

Matthew Chadwick, wheeling a single piece of

luggage, passed Susan as she left Lynette's office. He was a handsome man with neatly-cut hair and manicured nails and feet. She noticed his perfect toes in his leather sandals. He wore Bermuda shorts and a Lacoste polo shirt. *I've been to Mexico City in the fall. It's definitely not shorts-and-sandals weather. If he's right off the plane, where exactly did his flight originate?*

Chapter 4

When Susan arrived home, she took out her laptop and searched for flights from Mexico City. She'd noticed that Matthew Chadwick had an Aeromexico tag wrapped around the handle of his carry-on.

"Come on up, Ludwig." While waiting for the computer to turn on, she scratched his silky head, eliciting purring. "Want to help me solve a murder? We're looking up flights."

Aeromexico had only one direct flight, and it wasn't due to arrive until later this afternoon. *What's his game? Why would he lie about where he was?* She scrolled through other flights from the same airline. There was one that arrived from Puerto Vallarta at about the correct time, working backward to allow time to retrieve luggage and fetch his car before getting to the police station. *Maybe there's a satellite branch of his company there.*

She found the Agrowmex website, which did indeed have a branch in Mexico City, but none on the west coast of Mexico. In fact, the main plant on the outskirts of Mexico City was the only one in the country. *How do you take a business trip to a place where there's no business?*

She went as far as looking up businesses in and around Puerto Vallarta that sold farming equipment, supplies, and even construction materials. Zippo. It was a resort town. The main industries were fishing and tourism. *How about advertising agencies?*

Her slightly long nails clicked on the keyboard. Now

that she was retired and not playing the piano every day, she enjoyed bimonthly gel manicures. *I look like one of those society ladies who never wash her own pots.* Not that she did wash pots very often. Her cooking these days mostly involved the microwave.

Her search turned up a few small agencies that specialized in real estate, time-shares, and resorts. *Mexico City is a major business center. Surely he could have located an agency nearer the plant.* Her stomach growled. She hadn't realized it was lunchtime. Before closing the computer, she remembered the conversation with the emergency room doctor and typed WebMD into Google.

Type 2 diabetes. Symptoms include excessive thirst or hunger and frequent urination. She had been getting up several times a night to use the bathroom. And she was hungry all the time… *No wonder I couldn't stick to a diet. I'm fighting a disease.* She looked at the risk factors—genetics, overweight, lack of exercise… *I'm not that overweight, and I do manage to walk now and then. I'll bet I inherited bad genes from Audrey. Figures.*

She was about to blow it off until she read about the possibility of heart and kidney disease. She reluctantly took her phone out of her purse and called her primary care office, hoping it would be a while before they could squeeze her in.

"You have an opening tomorrow afternoon? Really? *Why did I have to wait two weeks for an appointment when I had that awful sinus infection?* Sure. Four o'clock tomorrow. No, my insurance hasn't changed."

She went into the kitchen and reheated leftover pizza in anticipation of a restricted diet soon to come.

Chapter 5

As usual, Susan woke up before the alarm went off. Mike was downstairs making coffee. She took a quick shower and threw on her new brown PajamaJeans trousers and a pumpkin-colored sweater.

Mike called up the stairs. "I'm making eggs. Want some?"

"Sure." She padded down the steps. She supposed it would be egg whites and fruit from now on, after this afternoon's doctor visit. Wait. She saw on *Doctor Oz* that fruit had a lot of sugar. *I refuse to eat vegetables at breakfast. I'd rather go hungry than scarf down broccoli at this hour.*

Mike handed her a plate. "Coffee's brewed. Are you ready to go back to school?"

"I am. I'm sure the gossip is flowing over there. I wonder if they have anyone to replace Melissa Chadwick—at least temporarily."

"I'm sure the principal has her hands full right now. A murder in an elementary school? You know, I wouldn't be surprised if parents start pulling their kids out like when that teacher was murdered at Annalise's preschool."

"It's bound to happen, at least until the murder is solved and parents feel safe about sending their kids again."

"Do you want me to meet you at your doctor's appointment?"

"No, I'll be fine."

"Write down whatever instructions he gives you.

And I'm willing to start our after-dinner walks again now that it's cooler." He kissed her good-bye, grabbing his black lunch pail on the way out.

When she arrived at Westbrook Charter, she noted the front parking area was busier than usual. She knew it had to be parents flooding the front office for information. She pushed her way into the office, grabbing her volunteer badge. The two receptionists buzzed around the front office like worker bees.

"Stephanie, what's happening? I'll bet Dr. Russo is swamped, especially now being down an assistant principal."

The secretary said, "She's got things under control. And we aren't down an AP. Larry Frisina was just appointed. You know him, right? He was the AP over at the elementary school. He was on the short list for the job when the school first opened."

"I remember. The salaries here are head and shoulders above what the public school employees are making. Guess that's a benefit of having a successful company funding the school."

Susan stopped to drop off her lunch in the teachers' lounge refrigerator, then headed for Theresa's fourth grade classroom. Walking into the classroom, no one would guess the school had just had a brush with a murder. The door read *Welcome* and was adorned with cutouts of fall leaves and pumpkins. Inside, the first thing to catch your eye was a canary-yellow bulletin board with pictures of the kids next to ghost stories they had written. Susan was happy to see that with the new push for reading and writing informational text, these kids still got to enjoy the thrill of writing stories.

"Hi, Susan. Are you doing okay? Jackson filled me in. You must have felt horrified thinking you'd killed someone." With her dark eyes and wavy black hair, there was no mistaking Theresa's Italian heritage.

Luckily, their son Ian took after Theresa rather than his father. Jackson had a good heart, but you'd never find his picture on a Hot Policemen's fundraising calendar. A flash image of a half-naked Jackson posing as Mr. January made her shudder.

"I'm relieved, as you can imagine," said Susan. "But poor Melissa! I can't fathom who would have wanted her dead."

"We all liked her even though she was inexperienced. Well, except that music teacher who comes in the afternoons. He's always talking dirt about the Chadwicks, what with Matthew the CEO of Agrowmex and Melissa walking into the role of assistant principal."

"Do you think he had it in him to commit murder?"

"Who am I to say?" Theresa lowered her voice to a whisper. "I've heard him say hateful things about immigrants and foreign businesses moving in. Robbing American jobs, how he was going to get even… stuff like that."

"Knock, knock." Theresa's next-door teaching neighbor came in with a stack of copies. "These were in your box."

"Thanks, Satin. Are you giving your reading pre-test today?"

"Yeah. Might as well get it over with." The diminutive redhead had a bright smile, revealing a gap between her front teeth. Susan wondered why her parents hadn't gotten her braces when she was younger. The sound of the bell pierced the room. "Another day, another dollar. See you at lunch."

Susan helped students with their seatwork while Theresa met with her reading groups. She kept looking at her watch, dreading the imminent doctor's appointment later that day. *Maybe I should replace my watch with one of those Fitbits.* As quickly as she thought it, she realized she didn't want alarms going off, telling her to get off the couch and move. Over the PA system, the principal announced a memorial service for Melissa Chadwick to be held the next day.

Theresa whispered in her ear. "Are you going? I'll bet most of the faculty will be there."

"Of course." Susan wanted to pay her respects. After all, she was the first to discover Melissa's death. And from past experience, she knew memorial services were notoriously good for observing people close to the deceased and picking up clues to potential suspects.

Theresa looked at the clock and began lining up her class for lunch. Susan walked with them to the cafeteria, and then she and Theresa entered the teachers' lounge.

"Are you all going to the service?" asked Satin.

The handful of teachers at the table nodded. Susan took her lunch out of the microwave and sat down. "Did you all know Melissa's husband, Matthew?"

Satin said, "He hung around during preplanning week, and he cut the ribbon when the school opened for business."

"Of course he did," said Stephanie, the receptionist. "He was all about the publicity."

Susan picked up on Stephanie's tone. "I'll bet he was a great help getting Melissa settled in her new job."

Stephanie made a face. "He was a help all right. When he wasn't flirting with me or one of the pretty, young teachers." She took a bite of her veggie wrap, shoving bits of lettuce and tomato out the other side and onto her napkin.

"Did he flirt with you too, Theresa?" asked Susan.

"Not once he realized I was married to a detective. Have to admit it was a little flattering, especially since I haven't yet lost all my baby weight and it's been almost a year."

"Is Ian doing better with the separation anxiety?" asked Satin.

"Not really. Had to peel him off me at the daycare again this morning. His teacher says he stops crying minutes after I'm out of sight. I don't stop till I'm in the school parking lot."

"They all go through it," said Susan. "Lynette had an awful time leaving Annalise when she was that age, but now that she's in preschool, she barely waves good-bye. Of course, now Mia is starting to enter that stage."

Theresa looked at the clock. "Lunch goes so fast. By the time you drop the kids off at the cafeteria, check your mail, and use the bathroom, you hardly have time to eat."

The afternoon went too quickly as far as Susan was concerned. *I shouldn't have worn this heavy sweater. It'll add at least two pounds to my weight this afternoon.* In the parking lot as she was leaving, she ran into the new assistant principal, just heading inside after directing parent pickup.

"Mr. Frisina, congratulations on your new position," said Susan.

He beamed like headlights in fog. "Thank you. We met at Antonio Petrocelli's Christmas party last year, didn't we?"

Surprised he'd remembered her, she said, "Yes, that's right. Will you be at the memorial service tomorrow?"

"Yes, I'll be at the memorial service. Melissa Chadwick was a fine woman and had the potential to become an influential leader. Such a shame."

His mouth said one thing while his body language conveyed the opposite. *Fine leader* indeed. She knew he had to be on cloud nine with his new position and higher salary. *I wonder if he has an alibi for the night Melissa was killed.*

She slipped into her Prius and drove under the speed limit to the doctor's office.

Chapter 6

The drive to her doctor's office should have taken ten minutes, but with determined procrastination, she stretched it to twenty. *They're never on time anyway. I'll just have to sit there for an hour before I'm seen.* She always marveled at the fact that given the size of Westbrook and its small population, on any given day that she'd been to her doctor, the office was full.

She walked through the heavy wooden door into the paneled office, signed in, and hunkered down in a well-worn chair. *Thank goodness for my Kindle app.* No sooner had she started reading one of the novels in her library, she was interrupted.

"Susan Wiles, haven't seen you in a while." A middle-aged, model-thin blonde took a seat beside her.

"Blair Cunningham? How have you been?" Blair had been a teacher at Susan's school years ago, but she'd quit to pursue a more lucrative career path selling real estate.

"Are Lynette and Jason enjoying the house?"

"Absolutely. You were right when you told them to go for a three bedroom. They have two daughters now and haven't outgrown it."

"I love finding the right house for my clients. Makes me feel kind of like a matchmaker."

"Well, I'm letting you know Lynette and Jason are still in love with it."

Blair's phone vibrated. "Excuse me. I have to take this." Blair walked to a remote corner of the waiting room. After a few minutes, Susan's mouth felt dry. While at the water fountain, she could hear Blair's end of the conversation.

"Yes, Puerto Vallarta. Beautiful. Okay, next week then." Blair was called into the examining room, not noticing Susan's back to her as she passed the fountain.

Puerto Vallarta. That's the second time in two days that city has come up. Was Blair meeting someone there? A boyfriend? Matthew Chadwick?

"Susan Wiles." The nurse, chart in hand, called her into the exam area and led her to the scale. She was going to step on it backwards so she wouldn't see the number, but given her personality, she couldn't bring herself to do it.

"You know, this sweater weighs a ton and I just ate lunch. Usually I only step on the scale in the morning." She kicked off her shoes and winced as the nurse pulled the metal balance out of the groove and slid it to the right. Twice. *She's making a face. Why are the nurses who weigh you always rail thin?* She was too old to use the, "it's that time of the month," excuse and opted instead for, "We had Chinese food last night, and it always makes me retain water." She could have sworn the nurse rolled her eyes. Happy to leave the scale, she followed the nurse into the exam room.

The nurse wrapped a cuff around her arm, then read the results. "Your blood pressure is a little high. The doctor will talk to you about it."

High blood pressure? Diabetes? She was in her early sixties and didn't expect to be falling apart so soon. A chart hanging on the wall showed something called A1C levels correlating to average blood sugars.

The door opened, and the baby-faced doctor, barely older than her son, Evan, read her chart and asked the same questions the nurse had just asked. He smelled clean, like he'd washed his hands with Ivory soap.

After listening to her heart and peeking in her ears and mouth, he scribbled notes on her chart.

"Well, Mrs. Wiles, we have a few serious issues to address. You'll have to change your diet dramatically and start exercising if you want to avoid taking medication. Diabetes can lead to kidney issues, blindness, sores that don't heal…"

She felt like a child being scolded by the teacher. What did he know anyway? She'd have to ask Evan if this advice sounded accurate. Then again, she wasn't sure she wanted her son to know how bad her eating and exercise habits had gotten.

"Take these pamphlets with you. Many of my patients find weight-loss success by joining a like-minded group such as Overeaters Anonymous."

Overeaters Anonymous? She was expecting him to say Weight Watchers or Jenny Craig. *Does he really think I'm a food addict?* She stuffed the pamphlets into her purse, vowing to find another doctor. Perhaps one who was older and stockier.

"The nurse will show you how to use a glucose meter. I'll call in a prescription for test strips. You need to check at least twice a day and keep tabs on the readings to see whether or not your revised eating habits and exercise schedule are effective. I'll see you in a month."

When she got home, she was greeted by the aroma of garlic and oil. Mike stood in front of the stove, holding a metal spatula above a sizzling pan.

"So what did the doctor say?"

"Just what'd you'd expect. I'm too fat, and I need to exercise." She grabbed a Pop-Tart out of the pantry. "And I had to get one of these! How am I going to get used to pricking my own finger?" She took the glucose monitor and lancet from her purse, sure that Mike had just winced while turning away from her.

"Let's take a walk after dinner. It's nice and cool out." Mike took clean plates out of the dishwasher and brought them to the table.

She didn't like this reversal of roles. Just a few years ago, it had been her nagging Mike to take walks after his heart attack. Now he was twenty pound lighter and *she* was the one with a health issue. "Did you hear from Lynette?"

"Yes. She said they got back the autopsy results. Melissa Chadwick's cause of death was strangulation."

"She was killed and then dumped off the railroad bridge. We thought as much."

"According to Lynette, that's what the coroner said. Lynette said she'd see you at the memorial service tomorrow." He drained the linguine and mixed it with the garlic and oil from the frying pan. "*Mangia.*"

Chapter 7

The sunny Saturday morning was perfect for riding a bike, going to a fall craft fair, or visiting a Farmer's Market. Being amidst mourners at a memorial service was at the bottom of Susan's list. Lynette knocked on the front door as Susan gulped down her coffee.

"Thanks for picking me up. No one likes going to these things alone," said Susan.

"I know. Did you eat a healthy breakfast?"

"Yes, like I always do. Can we talk about suspects?"

"I'm going to this service with you in hopes I'll get an idea where to start on our investigation. We know Melissa was strangled, then thrown off the railroad bridge at approximately nine p.m. Her husband didn't get back into town until the next morning, so he's not on our radar."

"Larry Frisina is sure to be there," added Susan. "It wouldn't be politically correct if he wasn't. He definitely benefitted from Melissa's death by getting to replace her as assistant principal and pulling a much higher salary than he was getting at Westbrook Elementary."

"You jump from *A* to *Z*. Just because he wanted her job, doesn't mean he had it in him to commit murder."

"He's an ex-marine. And he's kept himself in shape. Notice his biceps when you see him at the funeral." She followed Lynette to her car and slid into the passenger seat, hoping the conversation would stay centered on murder suspects rather than her diabetes.

"So, Mom. What did the doctor tell you?" Lynette

hadn't even made it to the main road before she asked.

"I have to watch my diet and exercise. I could have told you that."

"Do you have to take medication? Insulin?"

"I just have to keep tabs on my blood sugar for now. Hopefully diet and an exercise routine will do the trick." She wished she felt as casual as she sounded. She didn't want Lynette to worry, but in truth, she was terrified of going blind or losing a limb. *This time, I'm going to stick with a program.*

They drove past fiery-colored trees, around the mountain, and onto Huguenot Street. When they made the turn, they encountered an eclectic group of protesters carrying picket signs. When Lynette rolled down the car window, Susan heard them saying things like "no factory farming," and "immigrants go home." The church was just up the street. She was amazed at their audacity.

Lynette yelled at them, "You'll need to leave the area. There's a memorial service starting soon, and this is inappropriate."

Susan recognized Della Hops, her wild gray hair blowing in the breeze, tie-dyed T-shirt under a crocheted cardigan. "We're exercising our first amendment rights. You can't make us go."

Lynette said, "I can't make you, but I'm appealing to your sense of compassion. A woman is dead. She deserves a peaceful good-bye."

Della dropped her sign, and the other protesters followed suit. Lynette rolled up the window and proceeded to the church.

The parking lot was half-full. Melissa and Matthew Chadwick had been away from Westbrook for over a decade, and Susan expected most of the mourners would be from the school or Matthew's company. A blue pickup truck was parked on the swale. When they passed it, Susan noticed the driver slumped down in the seat, a baseball cap pulled over his brow. Shrugging off the incongruity, she followed Lynette into the church.

A dirge droned from the bell tower of the gothic-styled stone church. Susan pulled open the solid wood door, and she and Lynette chose a pew near the back. Matthew Chadwick sat in the front row with his son, Jordan. Jordan attended college at the state university just outside of town. Although within an easy commute, he shared an apartment with two of his buddies. Susan remembered Melissa mentioning that she thought it was a waste of money to pay rent for him when he didn't have to, but she was just glad he'd opted to return to the states rather than stay in Mexico City.

"Jordan must be heartbroken," said Susan. He was built like Evan—tall and muscular with wavy brown hair. The similarities between him and her son ramped up her empathy for the boy.

Lynette whispered, "I hope he straightens out now that his mother is gone. His father needs him."

"What do you mean by straightens out?"

"We picked him up a few times for drunk and disorderly conduct. College kids, Saturday night at the bars… nothing serious but enough to cause his parents concern."

"I imagine he's getting a business degree. He's guaranteed a job at Agrowmex with his father being CEO."

Blair Cunningham, in a tight black pencil skirt, her blond hair in a French knot, walked past them and slid into the pew behind Matthew Chadwick. She leaned over, her arm on his shoulder, and whispered something into his ear. It made Susan crazy not to be able to hear what she was saying. She still wondered about the Puerto Vallarta connection, and now she had proof they knew each other.

The priest led the group in a prayer. The principal of the new charter school spoke about how helpful Melissa had been in the short time since the school had opened.

Jordan followed. He spoke about the guidance his mother had given him and reminisced about going with her to the park and helping her stir cookie batter when he was small. Until this point, Susan hadn't noticed anyone—not even Matthew Chadwick—sobbing or shedding tears. She watched from behind, wondering if Matthew would pull out a handkerchief. Even now, he sat like a statue in the front pew, Blair right behind him.

Now it was Matthew's turn to speak. He rose from the pew, took a stack of index cards from his jacket pocket, and stepped up to the podium.

"My wife was a wonderful woman. A soul mate and life partner. She…"

There was an explosion, louder than a clap of overhead thunder. People screamed, heading for the doors. Someone stepped on Susan's foot while yelling about terrorists.

Lynette shouted, "Everyone stay calm. Walk calmly toward the exit." She couldn't be heard over the din that reverberated in the church.

A smelly gray smoke snaked through the aisles and filled the pews. There was coughing, screaming, and pushing that rivaled Black Friday.

"Lynette, what's going on? Someone said terrorism?"

"Yep. Terrorists love to target small town memorial services when they could be hitting up—oh I don't know—Rockefeller Center?" She dragged her mother away from the church. "We're all still alive as far as I can tell. The walls are still standing. Did you hear gunshots amidst the explosion?"

"More like a row of cannons doing a twenty-one-gun salute." Susan choked on the smoke. How did her daughter manage to stay calm, no matter what situation she faced?

"Come on, Mom. Take my hand."

The gray smoke made it nearly impossible to see. She labored to breathe. Lynette led her still farther from the church, then went back in to see if others needed help. By this time, Susan heard sirens and saw the blue pickup truck that she'd noticed earlier peel out of the parking lot. Her eyes were tearing too much to see the numbers on the license plate.

"My glasses!" She retraced her steps, finding her bifocals in the grass where Theresa and Satin were talking.

"Susan, are you okay? I... I saw Lynette go back in, but I think most of the people are out." Theresa coughed and wiped her eyes with her jacket sleeve. Susan watched a fire truck pull in, followed by a police cruiser and an ambulance. *Ambulance? I hope no one was hurt.* She scanned the crowd. *It looks like everyone made it out.*

"Do you think the furnace exploded?" said Satin.

"Just when Matthew was speaking? I don't think so," said Susan.

Lynette exited the church. She shooed the crowd farther away, then approached Susan. "Everyone made it out, thank God. Could have been much worse."

Susan noticed several people sitting on a stretcher near the ambulance, oxygen masks covering the faces of some. The EMTs checked for injuries.

"Did you see anyone suspicious in the church?" asked Lynette.

"No," said Satin. Theresa, agreeing with Satin, shook her head.

"I saw a blue pickup truck peel out of the parking lot just as we all came outside. It was the same one that was parked on the swale earlier. It was blue and looked like it'd seen better days. I tried to get the license…"

"It's okay, Mom. That's a great starting point. I'll have to hang out here for a while. Let me call Dad to pick you up."

"I'll drop you off," said Theresa.

Susan didn't protest. Mike would be worried sick if Lynette called and told him over the phone what happened. She'd rather him see her unscathed before she broke the news. She heard shouting and turned to see Jordan Chadwick storming past his father. Not a minute later, Blair Cunningham ran over and embraced Matthew. Susan hadn't seen Larry Frisina, the new AP, at all. She wondered if he drove a blue pickup truck.

Chapter 8

The next morning, Susan and Mike lingered over the Sunday paper.

"Here's an article about the smoke bomb," said Mike. "It's like Lynette told us—it was meant to create turmoil, but it wasn't designed to kill anyone."

"Half a dozen people were taken to the hospital because of the smoke. What a horrible thing to happen right in the middle of the service. I wonder if it will be rescheduled."

"The paper said those treated at the hospital have been released. That's good news. I hope you stay out of this, Susan. Whoever killed Melissa Chadwick means business."

Susan finished her oatmeal and started on the crossword puzzle. She'd skipped her walk last night. After coming home, all she wanted to do was curl up and watch the Hallmark channel. Her blood sugar was high this morning, and the last thing she felt like doing was exercising. She had an idea.

"Mike, how about we drive up to the craft fair today? It's supposed to be beautiful weather, and I can get in my exercise."

Mike looked up from the paper. "Yeah. We can go for a while."

Susan knew that was code for, "I can only take so much wandering around aimlessly, so let's keep it short."

After breakfast, they got ready and jumped into the car. The roads were empty, and the colorful trip up the mountain to the fair went quickly. The craft fair, *this* craft fair, occurred every October. It gave farmers and apple growers a chance to sell their last big harvests before winter set in. Susan often found Christmas presents here—last year she'd bought a quilt to send to Jonathan, her birth father, and a personalized cloth storybook for Annalise. *Maybe I can find a wooden puzzle that says Mia this year.*

"We're here," said Mike. He pulled onto the grass behind a truck.

As soon as they'd gotten out of the car, the aroma of hot apple fritters tantalized her resolve. *Just say no.* She grabbed Mike's hand, and they strolled in the opposite direction, past booths selling apple cider, honey, and homemade soap.

Mike stopped at a booth. "Veal cutlets? Since when do you see those at a craft fair?"

"Look, Mike. There's the toy booth. I want to get something for the girls." She found a pink step stool for Annalise and had it personalized on the spot.

Mike said, "Let's get this push toy for Mia. She'll be walking soon."

At the next booth, Della Hops and two of her cronies were selling corn, gourds, and pumpkins. Realizing Halloween was around the corner, Susan stopped to take a look.

"How's business going?" asked Susan.

"It's been better. I didn't bother trying to sell our apples this year, what with Agrowmex selling them at ShopRite for half the price I usually get." Della wore a Woodstock sweatshirt, which looked old enough to have been an original. Her frizzy gray hair was pulled into a messy ponytail. "You know, don't go giving those grandbabies of yours those apples or anything else that comes out of that factory. I know they're up to no good, making genetically modified produce." She mouthed *GMOs* in an exaggerated fashion. "That's how they can sell it so cheap. You can't tell me food that's been fiddled with like that is safe to eat."

"Della, you know I always buy from the local farmers. How much for three pumpkins?"

Mike whispered, "Three?"

"We'll carve one for our porch, and I'll let Annalise decorate one for herself and her sister."

Della motioned to the man in overalls to take the money and pack the pumpkins. "I saw the smoke coming from the church during the service. Everyone hates the Chadwicks and their business. That Mexican megafarm and its head honcho have got to be stopped before it's too late." Her words spewed venom. Wrist shaking, she handed Mike the burlap tote bag.

Did Della have anything to do with Melissa's murder or the smoke bomb? She'd seen her and her cronies protesting outside the service yesterday. Della didn't have the strength to kill Melissa and throw her off the bridge. She could barely lift the bag of pumpkins. Lots of strong farmers lived with Della on the commune, however, and they were all of like mind.

"Let's eat," said Mike. He led her to a food truck where they bought sausage and peppers sandwiches, then sat at a wooden picnic table to eat. Susan noticed Satin sitting at the next table with a handsome redhead.

"Great day for a fair," said Susan. Satin smiled when she recognized her.

"Sure is. Susan, this is my... friend, Trey Fisher."

He extended his hand to both Susan and Mike. He was wearing a Yankees shirt.

"Hi. I'm Susan Wiles. This is my husband, Mike. Mike, this is Satin Page from work."

"Too bad our team didn't get the wildcard spot in the playoffs," said Mike.

"Don't get him started," said Satin. "He's a huge

fan, and it hit him hard."

"Glad we're all alive and well after the service yesterday. Looked like most of the school was there. You know, I didn't see Larry Frisina there, did you?"

"Come to think of it, I didn't. Maybe he's sick," said Satin.

"You're probably right. New school year, new germs. And I'll bet he has some loose ends to tie up at Westbrook Elementary as well." Susan noticed Satin's necklace. "That's beautiful. Are those blue beads lapis?"

"Lapis alternating with smaller beads. You know I love artsy jewelry."

Satin and Trey finished their sandwiches and scooped up their trash. "See you tomorrow, Susan." Trey picked up a wooden coffee table.

"What a find," said Susan.

"It will be perfect in front of the new sofa I bought," said Satin.

After Susan and Mike finished, they headed back to the car.

"Mike, you know I've never even seen the Agrowmex plant. Isn't it on our way home?"

"More or less. What's there to see? It's a Sunday. Everything will be locked up."

"I know, but I want to be able to picture it in my head."

They drove down the mountain and turned onto a dirt road carved by tractor wheels. The sun sank lower behind the mountains. The Agrowmex plant was unremarkable. The flat-topped, cement building, surrounded by a wire fence, was windowless and sat on an expanse of farmland.

"Let's get out and have a look," said Susan. Mike followed reluctantly. "I'm guessing the crops are behind the building." She found an opening in the fence. *If I relax and fold myself like in yoga, I can fit through here.* She held her breath. *Made it.* Mike stepped through without effort. She led him toward the back of the factory, tripping on apples that had fallen to the ground. Mike grabbed her arm, preventing her from hitting the ground. They walked toward the edge of the woods, which abutted the land.

"Mike, they don't have livestock here, do they?"

Mike worked in the city permits office. "No, they're only zoned to grow apples, corn, and tomatoes."

Suddenly a loud boom broke, and they froze in their tracks. Mike grabbed Susan's hand. "That sounds like a shotgun."

Another boom, this time closer. Mike pulled Susan through the fallen apples and crunchy leaves, holding her hand as they ran toward the car. As they approached the hole in the fence, they heard one more gunshot, now deafening in its closeness.

Susan stepped into the hole, then tried to fold her body small enough to get all the way through. Her foot was stuck in quicksand-like mud. "Mike, I'm stuck." Her heart beat like a jackhammer inside her chest.

Mike put his hands on her butt and gave her a shove. She fell face down into the mud, but she was free. Mike stepped through and yanked her up. "Run, Susan."

This time they both heard a cow. "Come on, Mike. Let's see where it's coming from. Having farm animals on the premises is illegal, right?"

"Are you crazy? We have to get out of here." He pulled her toward the car. Another shot pierced the air. Mike started the engine and peeled out.

Susan's heart didn't stop racing until they got to the main road. "I'll call 911."

"And say what? We were the ones trespassing on private property. When we get home, let's call Lynette directly. I told you sleuthing was dangerous. I never should have agreed to stop here."

Chapter 9

Susan hummed to herself as she quickly dressed and got ready to go to school the next morning. Her mission: to see if she could uncover any new information about the bomb, the surprising findings at Agrowmex, or the whereabouts of newly-appointed assistant principal, Larry Frisina, the night Melissa Chadwick was murdered. Mike warned her not to say anything about the cows they'd heard at Agrowmex, and she agreed it was the smart thing to do. Let the police catch them red-handed before they have a chance to hide the evidence—although she couldn't imagine where they'd stash a bunch of farm animals.

Susan grabbed her volunteer badge, then peeked her head around the corner to Larry Frisina's office. Several teachers were enjoying a few minutes of socializing before the bell rang.

"Hey, did any of you see Larry Frisina?"

As she grabbed her mail, one of the teachers said, "His truck wasn't in the parking lot. Maybe he's still sick."

Susan stashed her lunch in the refrigerator and headed down the Halloween-decorated hallway to Theresa's room.

"Hi, Susan." Theresa stifled a yawn. "I sure appreciate your being here today. Ian kept me up half the night. Jackson sleeps like a log. I'm the one who drags herself out of bed whenever the baby beckons."

Satin popped her head in. "Theresa, do you have the sign-in sheet from open house? I forgot to get it from you last week."

Theresa grabbed a legal pad. "Here you go."

"Thanks for covering for me."

"An emergency is an emergency. You'd do the same for me." She noticed Susan sorting worksheet copies and smiled. "Wasn't the fair great? I'm so happy I found that coffee table."

"And it's a good thing your boyfr—your friend Trey was there to carry it. Looked like it weighed a ton."

"Yeah, and he has a truck. It never would have fit in my Nissan." The bell rang. "It's that time already. See you at lunch."

The kids rushed in like a herd of horses, as energetic as they were when Susan taught music. Some days she missed the kids. Other days she felt her age and couldn't imagine spending a whole school day being "on." Retirement had its perks.

While Theresa got the students started on their work, she motioned to Susan. "I'm short of copies. Can you run downstairs and make some more?"

"No problem." Susan took the stairs in an effort to sneak in some exercise. When she went into the copy room, she saw Larry Frisina go into his office, which was right next door. His phone rang, and rushing to get it, he left his door ajar. She wasn't eavesdropping but couldn't help overhearing the conversation.

"Yeah, I know. I thought I took care of this last week. It's a problem, I know. Yes. Of course, no one knows. It would be the end of my career. Should I come over? Okay, let me know if you need me."

The end of his career? Took care of the problem?

"Are you done with the machine?" The principal's secretary came up behind her, and Susan jumped. The six copies she needed to make were long since finished.

"Sure. I'll grab these and be on my way."

She returned to Theresa's classroom and circulated

amongst the various learning centers while Theresa worked with the reading groups. Checking her phone, she read a message from Mike. *Checked permits and blueprints. No record of a second building at Agrowmex. Called Lynette.*

No record of a second building, and they'd both heard cows. *Maybe there's more to worry about than GMOs over there.* When the company proposed moving into town, they'd promised no livestock, just produce. *If Della and her hippies got word of a company raising livestock for butchering at Agrowmex, there's no telling how violently they'd react.*

Theresa called the students to line up for lunch. "Come on, Susan. You look like you're a million miles away."

"Sorry. Did you say lunch?" She followed Theresa to the teachers' lounge.

"Guess what I saw this weekend?" said one of the teachers. "Matthew Chadwick with that blond real estate agent. The one who says she used to be a teacher."

This nugget of gossip had everyone at the table salivating. Theresa said, "Where?"

"They were coming out of Vinny's Saturday night. His wife's body is barely cold, and he's out in the open with another woman? What's this world coming to?"

"Do you think he was seeing her before Melissa died?" asked someone.

"I wouldn't be surprised," said Stephanie, the receptionist. "There's Mr. Frisina."

"Hello, ladies. Enjoy your lunch," said the tall, lean assistant principal.

Susan said, "I'm glad they brought you aboard so soon." *He doesn't look sick to me.*

"Melissa's death is such a tragedy, but the school must go on. Jordan Chadwick is in his mother's office–

–now my office—collecting her things. Matthew Chadwick contacted me about setting up a scholarship fund in Melissa's name. I need a volunteer to act as a liaison between him and the school. Any takers?"

Theresa said, "Susan, you'd be perfect for that job."

"That would be wonderful. What do you say, Mrs. Wiles?"

"I suppose I could fit it into my busy schedule. Sure, I'll help." Susan's phone vibrated. "Excuse me. I'll take this outside." She was always happy to hear Mike's voice.

"I went through the records, and according to the plans, there isn't a second building at Agrowmex, nor did they file a permit for livestock. I'm glad we changed our minds and asked for her help."

"Yes, I read your text."

"Lynette says she needs a warrant to search Agrowmex and doesn't have any tangible evidence to get one. She said if she's in the area, she'll drive by."

Susan peeked her head in the teachers' lounge. Theresa was already gone. She caught a glimpse of Jordan Chadwick carrying a carton of things out of Melissa's office and walked over to him.

"Jordan, I'm so sorry for your loss."

"You knew my mom?"

"Yes. I volunteer here at the school. As a matter of fact, I just agreed to work with your father to set up a scholarship fund in your mother's name. I saw you at the service yesterday."

"Can we count that as a service? Who sets off a bomb in a church during a funeral?" He slurred his words.

Susan's nose twitched. Jordan reeked of marijuana. "At least no one was hurt. You take care of yourself and your father."

Jordan left, and Susan returned to Theresa's

classroom. She set up the geo-boards, rubber bands, and tiles in the math centers. *Wish we'd had this stuff when I was a student.* Theresa stood in front of the class, writing on the dry-erase board. Halfway through the math lesson, one of the students started wheezing.

The students took it in stride. One said, "She's having another asthma attack."

"She has these frequently. Susan, can you take her to the clinic? She has an inhaler down there."

Susan led the girl to the clinic and waited to make sure she was okay after the nurse gave her the inhaler. Then she started to go back upstairs, when she saw Matthew Chadwick going into Melissa's office.

"Mr. Chadwick, I'm so sorry for your loss and about what happened at the church."

"Thanks. It's been tough, and I'm sure it won't feel better anytime soon."

"I was just talking to Mr. Frisina. I'll be helping you set up the scholarship in your wife's name."

"Great. Let's get together later this week. I came to collect Melissa's things from her office."

"I ran into your son earlier. He was here to do the same."

"Really? He has classes today."

"Did he mention he was coming here?"

"No, but we're not exactly on speaking terms at the moment. If you'll excuse me…"

I saw them fighting at the service. Wonder what it was about. Did Jordan find out his father was seeing another woman? Blair Cunningham cozied right up to Matthew at the church. Or was Matthew upset that Jordan was using drugs? Lynette said he'd been in some trouble in the short time he'd been in town.

Susan took a minute to use the faculty bathroom. When she came out, she heard Larry Frisina and Matthew Chadwick talking.

"I'm glad he's okay," said Matthew.

"He's not okay. The other day was a close call. If I hadn't gotten to him in time, he'd be dead. If you can't get your son in line, I'm going to the police."

"And how would that look? You have a new job and reputation to protect. I'm sure you don't want this getting out any more than I do."

"Did you find the 'proof' that Melissa was talking about? Thank God she never made it to the police."

"No. I'll go through what's left of her things. I hear Jordan was already here. He may have found it. It's not at home. I searched high and low."

"I've been pawing through her desk as well. Didn't find it."

"Take care of Chance. We'll keep this quiet. Meanwhile, enjoy your new post, which believe me, I'm taking slack for giving to you without opening it up to the public."

Larry's walkie-talkie radio sizzled. "It's an emergency on the field. Got to run."

Larry raced toward the door, and Matthew headed to the parking lot.

Proof? In his haste, Larry Frisina had left his door ajar. Susan inched down the hallway, monitoring right and left, seeing no one. She made an executive decision to check out Larry's office.

What sort of clue were Matthew, Larry, and Jordan, looking for? It had to be something incriminating but small enough not to be in plain sight. She ran her fingers across the books on the shelf, then pulled out a few to check behind. Nothing.

Next, she went to the desk, sparsely covered with a leather-rimmed calendar, a brass lamp, and a photo of a boy who looked to be in his late teens. *He looks like Larry. Must be his son.* Although it was the most obvious place to start, she'd once found a clue under a false drawer bottom. She carefully searched the bottom of each drawer to no avail. Then she pulled the drawers all the way out. *I've seen clues taped to the bottoms of drawers before.* Excitedly she peeked underneath but came up empty-handed.

Meanwhile, she heard an ambulance siren. Soon she heard an EMT asking where the emergency was.

"Out on the field," she heard Stephanie say. "The principal is out there."

Susan pushed a chair over to the tall bookshelf and warily ran her hand along the top. All she found was an inch of dust, which made her sneeze. She'd just climbed down and returned the chair to its original position, when she heard Larry's voice.

"Stephanie, I need an alternate phone number for the kid's parent."

"Is he okay?"

"Looks like a broken leg. Wait, never mind. I have it in my office."

Susan froze in her tracks. *Now what?* She felt her fight-or-flight hormones racing through her veins and opted for flight. Under the desk. She heard her knees creak as she bent down and curled up under the large oak desk. Holding her breath, she gambled on Larry being in a hurry and grabbing what he needed from the other side. The footsteps came closer. She felt another sneeze coming on. She held her nose trying to make the urge go away. It wasn't working.

Larry was now inside the office. She stuck her nose into her knees hoping it would stifle the inevitable sneeze that would surely give her away. Larry was right on the other side of the desk.

"I know I just saw a permission slip for him for his class field trip," Larry mumbled. He riffled through papers on the desk. Susan felt like her nose was going to explode. *God, please let him find the number. Now.*

"Ah, here it is." Susan heard him run out the door, then she let out a sneeze loud enough to wake the dead.

Chapter 10

By the time she got home, Susan's body said *nap*, but her mind said *research*. She changed into lightweight sweatpants and a long-sleeved tee, made herself a cup of pumpkin spice coffee in her Keurig, and settled down on the couch with her laptop. Ludwig snuggled up next to her.

"Ludwig, we're looking for information about Larry Frisina. Let's check public records."

She scrolled through pages of information, then found a record of a divorce. "This was fairly recent, Ludwig." She checked real estate records and found he had sold his house at around the same time as his divorce. *I think I'll give Theresa a call. She worked with him back at Westbrook Elementary after I retired.*

"Theresa, it's Susan. I was wondering, do you remember Larry Frisina going through a divorce? Really? So they did have a son... a troubled son. Drugs? Oh? His wife moved to New Jersey? Yes, I did hear that... No, I didn't know Blair Cunningham sold— What? Yes, his house. Does his son live here or with his mother? Thanks, Theresa. Kiss Ian for me."

So, Larry Frisina's son had drug problems and Theresa thinks he still lives in town. If so, he would have gone to Westbrook High. Time to call my contact.

Susan called her friend, Janet, a media specialist. Susan had volunteered regularly in the media center at the high school up until the time that Theresa asked her to help get her new classroom off the ground.

"Hello, Janet? I know, I miss you too, but I'll be

back as soon as Theresa gets settled. I was wondering if you remember a student named... actually, I don't know his first name. Last name is Frisina. He's the son of the new AP at the charter school."

"You're talking about Chance Frisina. He was a student here but got into trouble with drugs. He went off to rehab, then came home, but last I heard he relapsed and then had gone back for another stint. It caused a big strain on his parents. They wound up divorcing. Chance dropped out of school but I think he still lives in town."

"So Larry stayed, but his ex-wife moved away, right?"

"Yeah. To New Jersey, I think. They sold their big house on Orchard Road. Larry bought a small place for him and his son near here. Blair Cunningham handled it for him. She used to be a teacher."

"I remember. Thanks, Janet. Yes, Mia is a doll. Annalise treats her like she's her second mommy. Let's get together soon for lunch."

Chance Frisina had an addiction problem. Jordan Chadwick reeked of marijuana when I saw him at school, and Lynette said he'd been in and out of trouble. Was there a relationship between the two? Their fathers seemed to be covering something up, and Melissa had some sort of proof that threatened the two families.

She heard the key in the front door. "Mike, you're home early."

"I stopped by to see Lynette. She swung by Agrowmex, drove around a bit. Said she saw no signs of livestock."

"You and I know what we heard."

"Do you think it came from a neighboring farm?"

"What neighboring farm? There weren't any other farms for miles, seemed to me. Don't you remember how they bullied the owners near the property into selling so they'd have more land?"

"Yeah, you're right. Della and her gang staged a sit-in."

"More than one. And do you remember who owned the places?"

"One was that guy who teaches music, the one who made a big fuss about Mexicans taking our jobs—Duncan Sitwell. He finally caved in under the pressure."

"That's right! I forgot all about that. Duncan Sitwell. He teaches at Westbrook Elementary and comes by the charter school to give music lessons a few times a week. He's driving a BMW now. I don't think the Mexicans are personally affecting him!"

"The pressure to sell was steep. He has to be resentful even if he did cash in on the deal. I heard the land had been in his family for over a century."

Susan put herself in Duncan's shoes. He was pretty much forced to sell his land and was vocal about blaming immigrants for taking jobs from American citizens. The Chadwicks moving back to town with Agrowmex and the charter school opening both negatively impacted his life. She googled his name while she still had the computer on her lap. Ludwig rubbed against her arm while she typed.

"Mike, look what I found. This newspaper article from a few years ago has a picture of Duncan in the midst of a bar fight. And the guy he's punching sure looks Hispanic." She read the article and summarized it for Mike. "Six people, including music teacher Duncan Sitwell, were arrested when an argument broke out over a Colombian soccer game that was airing on the bar TV. Sitwell and two buddies insisted, and I quote, 'Monday night football is an American tradition not to be usurped by a frickin' pansy soccer game.' Can you believe it? A bar brawl over what game was playing on the TV?"

"I can believe it. Sports fans can get crazy. Throw in national pride and a couple of beers and voilà."

"So let's review what we know. Larry Frisina has a son with an addiction problem, and Matthew Chadwick's son reeked of pot the other day. Melissa Chadwick had information damaging to the Chadwick's son Jordan and harmful to Chance Frisina. Larry Frisina knew something Matthew wanted to keep buried, so Matthew appeased Frisina by appointing him assistant principal of the charter school practically minutes after Melissa's death."

Mike scratched his chin. "And you think Matthew Chadwick is involved with the blond real estate lady who used to be a teacher, right?"

"She comforted him at the service, and there's a Puerto Vallarta connection. Melissa could have found out, and that's the proof she wanted to keep hidden. If she and Matthew divorced, and he was cheating on her, she could have wound up a rich lady, and Matthew would have taken a huge financial hit."

Mike said, "But why would Larry care about Matthew having an affair?"

"You're right. Whatever Melissa had would have hurt both families."

Susan's phone vibrated on the coffee table. "It's my father."

Mike went into the kitchen. Susan heard the water running and hoped he was starting dinner. "Jonathan, how are you?"

"I'm doing great for an old man. I have a big surprise for you and yours. I'm about to make a plane reservation, but I wanted to check your schedule first. I was thinking of a little trip to New York next week before the winter weather sets in."

Susan's voice rose. "Really? We'd love to see you. I hear you made a hit with your new granddaughter last time you were here, when Mike and I were up in Vermont."

"That Mia is something special. So is Annalise. That one's going to grow up to be a lawyer, you wait and see. She makes a convincing case for everything she wants to eat, play with, or do. Of course, I'm a pretty lenient mark."

"I heard. We'd love to see you."

"I'll make a reservation at the Holiday Inn and let you know when I schedule my flight."

"Holiday Inn? What kind of nonsense is that? You're staying with us. Can't wait to see you. Lynette will be thrilled."

She ended the call, then found Mike tearing lettuce in the kitchen.

"Jonathan is coming for a visit next week." She rubbed her hands together in anticipation. "And I just thought of something. His birthday is next weekend. He'll be eighty, though he doesn't look a day over sixty."

Mike finished with the lettuce and broke a handful of whole-wheat pasta into the now steaming pot of water on the burner. Susan liked whole-wheat pasta well enough if it was smothered in Alfredo, but with sauce as thin as stewed tomatoes… not so much.

Mike said, "Sounds like an excuse for a party. Annalise will love that."

Susan thought about how lucky she was to have found her birth father after all these years. She thought about how wonderful it was to have the family together. Well, except for Evan. He'd be coming home from medical school for Thanksgiving at least. Then she thought about birthday cake. Chocolate layers with thick buttercream icing… Life was good.

Chapter 11

Schools never truly felt like schools when the halls were clean, quiet, and empty. Susan had always felt that way. She stopped at the office for her badge, then climbed the steps, counting the task as part of her daily exercise. Theresa and Satin were hanging out in Theresa's classroom before the school day started.

Theresa wore a comfortable dress, sensible shoes, and had her thick, curly hair pulled into a low ponytail. "Hey, Susan. You look extra cheerful this morning."

"I am. My father is coming next week. Lynette and I are making big plans for his eightieth birthday," said Susan.

"It's so great that you have the chance to know him after all those years," said Theresa.

"It'll be the first birthday we've spent together. The man I grew up with will always be my dad, may he rest in peace, but yes, I am glad. I'm really glad I found Jonathan."

Satin checked the cardboard box at the back of the room. "A few pairs of shoes," said Satin. She was collecting items for needy foster children. "You're lucky to have two father figures. Some of us never even had one."

A young, ebony-skinned teacher popped into the classroom. "Mr. Frisina is out there whining about supervision. Watch him make us start doing morning duty."

"Like we don't have enough to do," said Satin.

"We're all already here when he pulls his truck into the parking lot at the last possible second before the buses arrive," continued the newcomer. "No wonder his son is so lazy. Takes after him. I stopped by ShopRite the other day, and his son is stocking the shelves, so I ask him if there's any more Cherry Dr. Pepper in the back. First he pretends not to hear me. Next, he gets this annoyed look on his face. Then he saunters into the back slower than a tortoise on Ambien."

Susan turned to the young teacher. "His son works at ShopRite?"

"If you can call it working."

"And you say Mr. Frisina drives a truck? What color?"

"Light blue. Old thing. I guess with his new higher salary now here at our school he'll be replacing it soon enough. I sure would." The teacher moved toward the door. "See you at lunch. Oh, and Satin, I have a few items my kids brought in for your collection. Some sweatshirts and jeans." She held up an orangey-brown hoodie she'd been carrying. "This one matches your hair. You might want to keep it for yourself."

"Thanks, but I have a drawer full of sweatshirts, and there are kids out there with none. I'll get them after school." The bell rang, and Satin headed out after the other woman.

Theresa said, "Susan, remember how you didn't think Larry Frisina was at Melissa's service the other day? Satin says she saw his truck pulling into the parking lot, then he made a quick U-turn and headed right back out. Do you think he could have planted the smoke bomb?"

Susan thought about it. "I did see a blue truck parked outside the church, but I think it was still there when we evacuated the church. Something's going on between Larry, his son Chance, Matthew, and his son, Jordan.

Melissa knew about it."

Just then, students poured through the door and unstacked their chairs. Morning announcements, reading groups, art class—the morning flew by. At lunch, Susan ran out to her car to get the bag of socks she'd bought at Walmart for Satin's foster kid collection. In the parking lot, she spotted Larry Frisina's blue truck. *Should I or shouldn't I?* Her curiosity won. She scanned the parking lot—empty in the middle of the day. She crept over to Larry's truck and peeked in the windows. There were scattered papers and receipts on the passenger seat. When she pulled the door handle, she didn't expect it to open. Didn't everyone lock their car doors? When it swung out, she again scanned the parking lot to make sure she wasn't being watched. Then she carefully riffled through the stack of papers and receipts.

These receipts are mostly from fast-food places. A rumpled McDonald's bag was wedged behind the front seat. She found a pamphlet on the floor. It was from the hospital and listed support groups that included Alcoholics Anonymous, a Lamaze class, Overeaters Anonymous, and a drug addiction support class—Be Free, Live Clean!

On further exploration, she found a plastic hospital bracelet on the passenger side floor. It looked like it had been hastily cut off with a dull tool. She opened the glove compartment and noticed a pair of wire cutters, which she assumed had done the trick. She examined the bracelet. *Chance Frisina. And the date is the same as the day of the memorial service.*

She carefully put everything back in its place, rationalizing that she hadn't really broken into the truck. It was unlocked, after all. She backed herself out of the truck just in time to hear a car pull into the parking lot. She froze. *That's all I need is for someone to recognize me coming out of Larry's car. That's how rumors get started.*

She crouched next to the front tire and waited, not relaxing until she heard the chirping of a lock remote. She waited a bit longer. *What's this?* She'd grabbed on to the tire to help herself crouch down, and now there was dried mud on her hand. She scraped the tread and discovered more dried mud and dried straw. *Hay, like from a farm. I'm sure Larry doesn't moonlight as a farmhand. Where has this truck been?* She remembered seeing hay sprinkled along the road near Agrowmex. *Why was Larry at Agrowmex? Was he meeting with Matthew Chadwick?* The last time she'd seen the two together they were both at the school and didn't appear to be concealing the fact they knew each other.

She came away from this little jaunt with several new clues. Chance had been in the hospital at the time of the memorial service. Larry had a pamphlet for hospital support groups—and she was certain neither he nor his son were interested in Lamaze classes. And the truck had driven through an area with mud and straw fairly recently. It hadn't rained in days. *The rain would have rinsed the tires clean, right?*

She was almost at the front door of the school when she remembered the socks for the collection. Grabbing the Walmart bag from her car, she once again headed back to the school.

"What took you so long? Did you go to Walmart and buy the socks just now?" asked Theresa.

"No, just wound up talking downstairs. You know me."

"You're thinking about murder. I know that expression."

"I was wondering about Chance Frisina. Does he come around school ever?"

"I met him once when he stopped by to get money

from Mr. Frisina. I happened to be in the hallway outside Mr. Frisina's office and saw the exchange."

"I heard rumblings that Chance was taken to the hospital for a drug overdose."

"That's right. It was the day of Melissa's memorial service. The ladies in the office said they got the call at school from the hospital. Larry had just left for the church. Fortunately, they had his cell number and notified him before he went inside. Good thing, because you know he'd have turned off his phone before it started."

"So that's why Larry wasn't at the church." *Then his hightailing it out of the parking lot had nothing to do with him planting the smoke bomb.*

"Speaking of murder, I wonder if Jordan Chadwick had an alibi for the night his mother was killed. He's strange. Hung around here with Melissa during preplanning, and there was always tension. I know they argued about how many classes he should take and when he planned to graduate from college, stuff like that."

"Can you mention that to Jackson? If Lynette hears it from him, she'll take it more seriously than if I tell her."

"Sure. Now let's see if we can get these kids to use water and food coloring without making a mess. Hands-on science—gotta love it."

After school, Susan made a detour. There was little in the house for dinner besides pasta. She'd been watching her diet a bit more carefully, and her blood sugar readings were down. Lean steak and baked potato sounded good. She'd surprise Mike and have it ready when he got home. Besides, maybe she'd run into Chance Frisina at ShopRite.

She arrived just before the pre-dinner rush. She filled her cart with lettuce, potatoes, cucumbers, and a bag of sugar-free peanut butter cups. With Halloween right around the corner, candy was everywhere, tempting her like the serpent in the Garden of Eden. *I will need some candy for the trick-or-treaters.* She threw a bag of fun-sized Snickers into her cart. A familiar blonde called to her from the end of the aisle.

"Hi, Blair." Glancing into the realtor's cart at multiple bags of candy, she said, "I see you're preparing for Halloween too."

"Hope I'm not overdoing it. I'm going on a business trip the day after Halloween, but I suppose the leftovers will keep."

"Business trip? I'll bet your sales are up here in town with Agrowmex opening."

"It's slowed down here in town, but many of the upper-management workers are looking for vacation homes, so I'm seeing a secondary boom. Have to ride it while it lasts. The real estate business is fickle."

"Poor Matthew Chadwick. He bought that beautiful home off Waffle Hollow Road, and now he's lost his wife before they could fully enjoy it."

Blair looked down. "Such a sad circumstance. What's this world coming to?" She shook her head. "Good seeing you. Have a nice evening."

Susan saw a flush of sadness wash over Blair's face when she mentioned Matthew losing his wife. Was it guilt? Not that Blair killed Melissa, but perhaps guilt that she'd been having an affair with Matthew. Flying out on a business trip? Would have been easy to have Matthew tag along on one of those trips. *I wonder if Matthew is going out of town this week as well.*

She rolled the cart down the cookie aisle, resisting the temptation to throw a bag of Oreos on top of the candy. Remembering why she was there, she headed to the meat case, where she rummaged through packages of steaks. She remembered the veal cutlets Mike saw at the fair and wondered if ShopRite had any. *Veal cutlets? Nah. I've rarely known this store to carry veal.* She recalled one of Della Hop's demonstrations when Henri's five-star restaurant opened in town. Due to the pressure and bad publicity Della had generated, Henri's took veal off the menu.

She felt a tap on her shoulder. "Planning a special dinner?" said Satin. She was with the redhead fellow from the craft fair.

"Thought I'd surprise Mike and make a home-cooked meal." She was sure it would be a surprise, especially if it didn't turn out like shoe leather the way her last attempt had.

"This store is a little out of the way, but they have better meats than the Safeway on Waffle Hollow. Trey and I thought we'd grill a nice rib eye before the winter sets in."

"Sounds like a fun evening. You should pick up a bottle of wine on your way out."

"Done," said Trey.

Susan went through the express lane and out to the parking lot. She spotted a blue truck like the one Larry Frisina drove parked near the entrance. *Enough thinking about Larry, Matthew, Blair, and murder.* Instead, she debated the merits of a steak rub versus a marinade while she drove home.

Chapter 12

Walking into school the next day, Susan thought about the wonderful evening she and Mike had last night. The steak melted in her mouth like butter, one of the best meals she'd cooked in some time. Her mom always said the way to a man's heart is through his stomach. After dinner, they'd taken a walk through the neighborhood, then cuddled on the couch and watched a movie. She ran into Satin in the mailroom, collecting a box of donations.

"How's the clothing collection doing?" asked Susan.

"It's going great. Even better than last year at my old school."

"That boyfriend of yours is pretty cute. Is there a future there?"

Satin blushed and changed the subject. "Are you ready for today? It's Halloween. You know what that means. A sweet-laden party this afternoon and a costume parade this morning to get the kids good and hyper. I should have used one of my sick days."

"It won't be so bad. They do look adorable in their costumes. It's tomorrow that'll be bad, after a night of eating candy and getting to bed late."

She and Satin walked up to Theresa's room. Theresa was dressed like Snow White and was sorting candy into orange and black goody bags.

"Where's your costume, Satin?"

Satin pulled a black headband with cat ears out of her bag. "I'm going minimalist this year. Did you put Ian in a costume for daycare?"

"Yep." She pulled out her phone and scrolled through a dozen pictures of Ian dressed like a Dalmatian. Susan oohed and ahhed, looking forward to seeing her granddaughters dressed up tonight.

At midmorning, Theresa lined up her class and joined the others for the parade. Susan watched from the sidelines. This was one of the parts of teaching she missed. As a music teacher, she hadn't been responsible for parading a class through the halls. She had instead been a spectator, watching every child in the school march in their costumes. *And I never had to serve sticky cupcakes and juice. They did that with their classroom teachers.*

She found herself standing next to Larry Frisina. "Aren't they cute?"

Larry smiled. "Too bad they can't stay little forever. I think back to when Chance was in elementary school. The biggest problems he had were forgetting his lunch box or learning his times tables. Then they grow up and you know what they say… big kids, big problems."

"I remember like it was yesterday, taking Lynette and Evan trick-or-treating. Now I have two grandchildren! This will be the youngest one, Mia's, first Halloween."

"Grandchildren. I hope the day comes when Chance is mature enough to be a father. Hey, look at that boy coming around the corner. He's dressed like a paparazzi. And the girl in front of him is dressed like Kim Kardashian!"

"In my day, it was superheroes and princesses. Reality TV stars hadn't yet been born." She looked at the boy's camera, and an idea struck her. *There are no security cameras on the railroad bridge where Melissa fell, but did the police check gas stations along the way?* She couldn't wait to call Lynette and ask. Maybe they'd spot a blue truck heading that way.

When the kids got back into the classroom, Satin brought her class to Theresa's room and they turned on a Halloween video.

"Theresa, did Jackson mention whether or not the police searched closed-circuit TV or security cameras the night of Melissa's murder?"

"I know he said he *wished* the bridge had a security camera, why?"

"I wonder if they backed up and checked out gas stations and ATMs. The murderer came to the bridge with Melissa's body. Do you think they'd spot a blue truck along the way? Larry Frisina doesn't have an alibi, does he?"

"Yes, in fact he does. Westbrook Elementary had its open house the same night we did. My friend who's still teaching there said Larry stopped into her classroom. He made the rounds while the parents were there."

"What about his son? He could have been driving it. I heard Lynette talking on her phone to Jackson right after the murder, and she said something about a witness passing a truck around the time the body was dumped. It was dark, the witness said, but he thought it was blue or black."

"If they find footage, they'll be able to see the plate number."

"And trace it to the owner—or owner's son."

Satin said, "That road leading to the bridge is pretty desolate. I can't imagine any cameras near there."

Theresa said, "It's worth a try."

After school, Susan hurried home to start preparing dinner. Trick-or-treaters typically came out early in her neighborhood. She poured candy into a bowl and put it on the table near the door just as Mike came in.

"Can't wait to see the girls in their costumes," said Mike. "Is Mia old enough to eat candy?"

"I bought her a sugar cookie at ShopRite. I don't want her choking on candy. Not that Lynette would let her near anything harmful. I swear she's more overprotective of Mia than she was with Annalise."

Susan and Mike ate a quiet dinner. Before the plates were cleared, Lynette and Jason stopped by with the girls. Annalise was dressed like a pirate, and Mia wore a puppy costume, which doubled as pajamas.

Susan and Mike both grabbed their phones to take pictures. Susan said, "I can't believe how adorable you girls look." She scooped up Annalise.

"My phone is vibrating," said Lynette. She handed Mia to Jason and walked into the kitchen.

Susan inched toward the kitchen, carrying Annalise. She could hear Lynette on the phone.

"Really? You have the bank statement and withdrawal slip. That's quite a sum, $200,000. What about the exchange rate? You have the transaction where he exchanged it for pesos. Yes, he said he was in Mexico City the night Melissa died, but I couldn't verify he was there. Not one person remembered a meeting with him. Get him in for questioning first thing in the morning. Thanks, Jackson." She rounded the corner just as Susan hustled back to the living room.

"That was Jackson. I'll deal with it in the morning," said Lynette.

"Lynette, did you check the area for security cameras? I know there weren't any on the bridge itself but maybe on the way to the bridge."

"Mom, of course we did. The blue truck the witness saw wasn't Larry Frisina's if that's where you're going. Larry Frisina has an alibi. He was at Westbrook Elementary all evening. We have a dozen parents who verified it."

"What about his son, Chance?"

"He was working at ShopRite that night. His

manager confirmed it."

"But the blue truck?"

"Doesn't belong to Larry or Chance. Besides, the witness wasn't even certain of the color. Let's forget about work and take some pictures of the girls. Then let's do a little trick-or-treating."

Lynette put the girls' jackets back on and headed out with Jason and Susan. Mike opted to stay home and answer the door. Their neighbors were mostly elderly, and seeing the girls lit up many faces. Annalise's plastic Jack-o'-lantern was nearly full by the time they reached the end of the neighborhood and headed back to Susan's. Mia had fallen asleep on Jason's shoulder, clinging to him like a baby koala.

When they got back to the driveway, Susan saw a note stuck to her windshield.

"What's that?" said Lynette.

Susan unfolded the note. As she read, her mouth tensed.

"It's a threat. It says to stop interfering, or I'll be the next one dropped from the bridge." She felt her hands tremble. Then she noticed a person in a red sweatshirt and clown mask hiding behind a tree. "Come here. Did you write this?"

Lynette put her hand on her mom's arm. "Mom, don't. Go inside. I'll talk to him."

The clown figure darted from behind the tree like a gazelle and flew across the street.

"He must have left it. Get him, Lynette."

Lynette took off down the road, gaining on the clown as he leapt over driveways and across lawns. She'd almost caught up with him, when she was blocked by a slow-moving vehicle full of teenage trick-or-treaters.

Susan yelled, "Get him, Lynette!" The trick-or-treaters laughed at the scene. Susan squinted to keep

Lynette and the clown in sight. "Come on, Lynette!" Jason tried to nudge Susan toward the door. "I don't see him anymore."

Lynette returned out of breath. "He had too much of a head start. I'll take the note, and maybe we'll get some prints."

Jason shifted Mia to his other side. "It's Halloween. I'll bet it's just a prank."

Lynette said, "If he hadn't mentioned the railroad bridge and targeted my mom, I'd agree. This is more than a prank."

Chapter 13

Susan tossed and turned, finding it difficult to fall asleep. A threatening note delivered by a clown on Halloween night, a mooing cow at Agrowmex, despite the company not having a livestock license, a mysterious clue hidden in Melissa's office, two shady young men, and now Matthew has withdrawn a large sum of money. For what?

She rolled over and debated whether or not to wake Mike and talk it out. He was snoring peacefully, so she opted not to. *Think of something pleasant. Jonathan would soon be in town.* She planned a menu for his birthday dinner, hoping Lynette would agree to do the cooking. She'd invite Theresa and Jackson, maybe Janet from the media center too. Before she knew it, Ludwig and Johann were nudging her to wake up and serve breakfast.

Mike rolled over and turned off his alarm. "Restless night?"

"I'm not happy about the threatening note. I must be too close to figuring out who killed Melissa."

"I know you feel a sense of responsibility since you found Melissa, but honestly, do I have to say it again? Let Lynette and Jackson handle it."

Susan turned on the TV on the dresser. "Hey, that's Matthew Chadwick's place on the news. See all that graffiti on it? Big red letters. It says *No factory farming. Murderer.*"

"Is he a murderer because he killed his wife or because he has livestock on his property?"

"Maybe both. The money he withdrew from the bank—maybe it was to use toward his business. He could be planning to expand the company."

Susan's phone vibrated on the nightstand.

"Jonathan, what a nice surprise. Can't wait to see you. What? You are? That's wonderful. No cab, we'll pick you up."

Mike said, "Did Jonathan move up his visit?"

"Yes. A meeting he was staying in town for was canceled, so he changed his flight. We can pick him up this afternoon."

She called Theresa and told her she wouldn't be coming into school. Instead, she spent the morning cleaning the house, making up the guest room, and stocking the fridge. Mike put in half a day at work, arriving home just after lunch.

"The house looks great. Excited to see Jonathan?"

"I can't wait to see him. I didn't tell Lynette. I thought I'd invite them over later and surprise her and especially the girls."

"Do you think Annalise is old enough to remember their last visit?"

Her phone rang. "Hello, Mr. Chadwick. Sure, I'd be happy to. Yes, I know where your house is. I'll be there."

"I assume that was Matthew Chadwick."

"Yes. He wants me to come by his house tomorrow to work on his wife's memorial scholarship."

"That's good. It will help him heal."

And keep me out of trouble. That's what he's really thinking.

Driving to LaGuardia was the usual traffic nightmare, but eventually Mike found a parking place. They were waiting at the gate when Jonathan arrived. Susan marveled at how fit and handsome he looked. Both he and her birth mother looked years younger than their chronological ages. Susan could only hope she'd inherited those genes. She gave him a hug.

"It's so good to see you. What a nice surprise getting to see you earlier than we thought."

Mike shook his hand. "Has it been cold in Atlanta?"

"It's getting there. Hope we avoid the ice storms and traffic monstrosity we had last winter. Commuters stuck on the roads all night long. Atlanta doesn't handle winter weather well."

Mike grabbed Jonathan's suitcase and wheeled it to the car. "How long are you staying?"

"About that—I have something to discuss with the family."

Susan's radar went off. *Discuss what? Is he ill? Is he revising his will?*

"What is it you want to discuss?"

"We'll get to that later."

"Lynette and Jason are coming over for dinner tonight."

Jonathan's eyes brightened. "I can't wait to see them. And I've missed my great-granddaughters terribly."

It was rush hour, and the ride home was excruciatingly tedious. Susan was anxious to get Jonathan settled and start dinner before the gang arrived. She couldn't wait to see the surprise on their faces when they saw Jonathan.

"Susan, what have you been up to these days? You're volunteering at the new charter school you told me."

"Yes, with an old colleague from my pre-retirement days. Theresa Simpson—I've mentioned her before. She's married to Lynette's partner, Jackson."

"Yes, you did. Any new cases come your way? I have to admit, working with you to clear my brother and get him out of jail got my juices flowing even if he's the same schmuck he always was."

"Oh my God, what do you think about him and Audrey getting married?"

"She's seeing his true colors."

"You've been in touch with Audrey?"

"She called to cry on my shoulder a few times. She figured since Richard's my brother, I'd have some great insight as to why he's such a jerk. You know, was he bullied at school? Beaten by my father?"

"You grew up in the same house, and look how wonderfully you turned out."

"Thanks, Susan. I told her a leopard doesn't change his spots. She should cut her losses and get out while she still can."

Susan changed the subject. "You asked about new cases?"

Even in the dusk, Susan couldn't miss the glare Mike shot her way.

"Yeah. Sounds like you're working on something. I can tell from the excitement in your voice."

"The assistant principal at the new charter school was murdered. I was driving home from open house, and this body came flying out and landed on top of my car."

"No, you're kidding. A body?"

"At first I thought I'd killed her, but Lynette says she was dead before she went flying off the railroad bridge."

She continued relaying all the details and rattling off her suspect list. Jonathan nodded his head and urged her to keep talking.

"You know, Susan, murders are most often committed by someone close to the victim. My money's on her husband or son."

Mike pulled into their driveway. "Susan knows her daughter and the rest of the Westbrook police force is the cream of the crop, so she can trust them to solve the case without her help. She failed to tell you about the threatening note she received on Halloween night and Lynette chasing down the street after a guy in a red sweatshirt and a clown mask."

Susan took Jonathan to the guest room, where Johann was curled up on the bed.

"I put fresh towels out for you, but if you need more, let me know. And there are two pillows on the bed—one firm, one soft. Just like the Hilton."

"You didn't need to go through so much effort, but thanks."

He plopped his suitcase on the bed and followed Susan downstairs, where she popped the ziti she'd assembled earlier into the oven. Mike tossed together a salad while Jonathan set the table. Susan slipped into the bathroom to check her blood sugar.

Soon they heard a knock. The front door opened, and Annalise ran into the kitchen, right past Susan, and grabbed Mike's leg.

"Grandpa, pick me up."

Never mind me, Annalise. Mike was her favorite grandparent, and she couldn't deny she felt a tad jealous.

Mike scooped her up. "Hey, sweetie." He smothered her with noisy kisses, causing her to giggle like the Tickle-Me-Elmo they'd gotten for Evan one Christmas.

Lynette said, "I picked up a pumpkin pie on the way. The stores are stocking them since Thanksgiving's right around the corner. I also bought a sugar-free cheesecake for you, Mom. How are you feeling? Has your blood sugar come down?"

"I'm fine, Lynette." She rolled her eyes. "It's under control."

She knew she'd been inconsistent with her health regime. She had to grab the bull by the horns and stick to a healthier diet, but lately—well, maybe for some time now—she lacked the willpower. Looking at her lively granddaughters and Jonathan, healthy and fit at his age, she made a vow to follow up on joining Weight Watchers. She'd already checked out the meeting schedule, planning on joining after the new year, but at the rate she was going, she'd be ten pounds heavier and even more diabetic before then.

"I'll take the ziti to the table," offered Jason.

Susan heard Jonathan coming down the steps. Annalise squealed. "GrampGramp!"

"Hey, pumpkin! I'm glad you remember me." Jonathan scooped her up and gave her kisses. Mia clung to Lynette.

"Mom, I thought Jonathan wasn't coming until next week? What a nice surprise."

Jonathan gave her a hug. "I was able to get away sooner than I thought. I have a surprise for you all, but I'll tell you over dinner."

Patience wasn't Susan's greatest virtue, but she put on a smile and got everyone seated at the table. Mike served the ziti. Lynette caught Jonathan up with Annalise and Mia.

"Last time I saw Mia, she had just started crawling. I'll bet she'll be walking soon."

"Soon enough," said Jason. That's when the fun begins."

"Tell us your news, Jonathan. I hope it's good news."

"Yes, Susan, it is. I've decided to retire for good this time. I put my place in Atlanta on the market, and I'm going to live out my golden years with my family. While I'm here, I was hoping you all could put me in touch with a good realtor."

Susan's eyes shone with delight. Blair Cunningham came to mind. "I do know someone," said Susan. "And

I'm thrilled that you'll be living here."

Lynette, Jason, and Mike echoed the feeling. Even Annalise seemed to understand that GrampGramp would now be more accessible. They gobbled up seconds before Mike brought out dessert. Susan felt a warm glow. After all these decades, she'd be able to see her birth father whenever she wanted to. After her meeting with Matthew Chadwick tomorrow, she'd call Blair Cunningham. The sooner Jonathan found a place in Westbrook, the better.

Chapter 14

The next morning, Susan's keen nose detected the aroma of pumpkin pancakes. She threw on her robe and padded down the stairs in her fluffy pink slippers. Jonathan and Mike were eating breakfast.

"Come join us," said Mike. "I made plenty of pancakes. And there's fresh Vermont maple syrup left from our last visit with Emily and Henry."

I'll check out Weight Watchers tomorrow. She pricked her finger and was disappointed to see how much of a bad effect last night's meal had on this morning's blood sugar reading.

"Jonathan, did you get a good night's sleep?"

"Absolutely. And when I checked my phone this morning, I had a voice mail from my realtor in Atlanta. A couple put a bid on my place. I didn't expect things to move so fast."

"That's great. I have a meeting this morning, but when I get back, I'll take you to meet the realtor I know here in Westbrook."

Susan got herself together and went over to the Chadwick place. It was a sprawling stone house with an expansive, dead lawn full of half-bare trees, littered with crunchy, colorful leaves. She walked up the sidewalk and rang the bell. Her sock had fallen into her boot, and she bent down to pull it out.

Matthew opened the front door. "Can I help you?"

"No, I'm fine." Embarrassed, she stumbled to her feet and followed Matthew into the living room where she sank into the leather sofa. "I think establishing a scholarship is a wonderful way of memorializing Melissa."

Matthew sat next to her. "It won't bring her back, but I'm doing something she'd be proud of." Matthew took out two legal pads. "I don't know where to start. I was hoping you'd give me some ideas."

"You could give it to a deserving fifth grader to use for college later, or you could award it to a graduating senior at Westbrook High."

"Melissa worked with the little ones. I like the idea of giving it to a graduating fifth grader. How about I split it—one for a boy, the other for a girl. I want to call it the Melissa Chadwick Memorial Scholarship."

Susan jotted down notes on the legal pad. "That sounds lovely. What criteria do you want to use to award it? Good grades? Citizenship?"

"Citizenship. Hmmm, I like that idea. Do they have some sort of elementary school graduation?"

"They aren't allowed to call it a graduation, but they have a commencement ceremony at the end of the year where they present awards."

Matthew stoked the crackling fire. On the mantel above the fireplace were family pictures and an antique clock.

"Those are lovely photos. I'll bet they bring back warm memories."

"You know, there's one missing. Very odd. When I came home the day after Melissa died, it was gone. The garage door wasn't locked. Melissa never went out without locking all the doors."

"Really? I hope you told the police."

"They shrugged it off. When I suggested Melissa may have been killed here at home, they said there was no evidence of a struggle, and her phone and purse were gone. They never did recover them. It bothers me because her car was parked in the garage. Her phone and purse weren't at home or in the car. The police haven't found the primary crime scene, although they say she was dead before being thrown off the bridge."

"If there wasn't a sign of a struggle, she must have been picked up by someone she knew in their car, or she could have taken an Uber or went for a walk."

"I'm certain she'd never heard of Uber, and she wouldn't have gone for a walk by herself after dark. The police spoke to all her friends, and no one saw her after she left the open house. Who could she have gone with? She didn't talk about friends outside of those she knew from school."

"Did the neighbors see anything?"

"They weren't home that night. And another thing— we got several calls in the weeks before Melissa died, but when we answered the phone, the person hung up." His phone rang. "Excuse me, I'll take this out on the porch. The reception is better. Make yourself at home."

Make myself at home indeed. Is he telling the truth, or did he kill his wife? If he did, he was a convincing actor. She walked over to the roll top desk and picked up a framed photo. It was a wedding picture. *They both look so young.* Then she thumbed through the appointment book sitting on top. *Old school, like me. I still like my calendar for keeping track of appointments.* She looked at the weekly calendar, where she saw an upcoming meeting with either an eight or an *S*, maybe a capital *B* penciled in a square. She heard the porch door creak and scurried back to the couch.

Matthew came in and set the phone down on the coffee table. "Business. You can never escape it when you're the CEO. I think we've accomplished a lot this morning. Thank you."

"I'll run it by the principal and get back to you. I'm sure she'll love the idea."

She got back into her car. *If he didn't love his wife,*

why keep family photos and a wedding picture in plain sight, especially if he's carrying on with another woman. His wife is dead. What's the point? And who is he meeting at eight? If it is business, surely his secretary has it on his work agenda.

When she got home, Jonathan was ready to go. He had printed listings of available houses from Zillow and had circled a few ads in the classified section of the paper.

"I'm glad to see you're eager! The sooner you move here, the better as far as I'm concerned. Did you talk to your Atlanta realtor?"

"Sure did. I accepted the offer, and she'll get the ball rolling."

Susan and Jonathan hopped into the Prius. "Blair's office is downtown on Main Street."

She pointed out the grocery store, post office, and Walmart along the way, hoping to orient her birth father to his new town. She passed the municipal parking lot and wondered if she should pull in or search for street parking. She was feeling lucky and opted for the latter.

"Impressive parallel parking, Susan."

"My dad taught me. He wouldn't let me take the driving test until I passed his test, and believe me, it was much harder." She wondered if Jonathan felt uncomfortable when she mentioned her dad. By the look on his face, she decided he didn't. "Here we are."

Blair's real estate office was nestled between the bank and a candy store. It was painted white with green trim. A bell tinkled when they walked through the door, announcing their arrival.

Blair, dressed in a tweed skirt suit accessorized with a strand of pearls, shook Jonathan's hand and introduced herself.

"Come, have a seat. You're going to love Westbrook. It's a charming, small town, but in less than two hours you can be in the heart of Manhattan with all the city has to offer. Tell me the nonnegotiables. For instance, do you insist on a modern kitchen, a big yard, near shopping?"

"I brought along some ideas." He handed her the classified ads he'd circled and pulled out the listings he'd printed from the Internet.

Blair took a few minutes to look through the ads. "Looks like you favor a two- or three-bedroom place, small yard, newish construction."

"Yes. I don't want a place that I have to worry about replacing the appliances or the roof. And although I wouldn't mind a small garden, I don't want a large yard to mow in the summer. While we're at it, not too big of a driveway to shovel in the winter either."

"A lovely new development went up when Agrowmex moved in. There are still a few places available. Let me pull up the listings."

Blair scrolled through, then printed several listings, which she handed to Jonathan. Susan looked over his shoulder while he read.

"New business from Agrowmex employees is dying down, now that they've been open several months."

"What do you do then? Westbrook doesn't have a high turnover rate. Most of the people I know have lived here their whole lives."

"Believe it or not, I'm doing a booming business selling vacation homes, especially in Mexico where many of the workers still have relatives."

Susan took the listings from Jonathan and flipped through.

"These look perfect. And they're within minutes of our house. Can we see them?"

"If Jonathan is interested, I'll go and get the keys."

Jonathan nodded, and Blair disappeared into the back. A second desk was neatly stacked with legal pads and mail. The other realtor was either off today or out showing houses. Susan couldn't help nosing through the papers on Blair's desk.

"Look, Jonathan. It's a check from Matthew Chadwick."

Jonathan took a look. "It's dated weeks ago. And look at the notation on the check. It says *Puerto Vallarta house.*"

"Do you think he was buying a love nest for him and Blair? He withdrew another large sum of money recently."

"I don't think you can jump to that conclusion. Sit down. I hear Blair."

"We're all set." Blair led them out to her car. "It isn't far. There are three properties available in that development."

Jonathan chatted with Blair, discovering she'd gone to school in Atlanta before her family moved to Westbrook when she started high school.

"Susan can tell you the schools here are excellent and always have been."

She continued to sell the town during the ride to the development. They passed Agrowmex and pulled into a gated community called La Puebla. Blair showed her credentials, and the guard waved them on. The road was flanked with young trees tied to wooden stakes, which supported the thin trunks.

"Give it a few years and those trees will shade the sidewalks nicely."

Susan hated to think it, but she doubted Jonathan would live long enough to benefit from the shade the trees would provide. For that matter, she doubted she would either.

Blair pulled into the driveway of a cookie-cutter brick house with white trim.

"I can't wait for you to see this. I think you'll love it.

Brand new, appliances are all under warranty."

Jonathan and Susan followed her into the living room. To the right of the door, a hallway led to three small bedrooms.

"The master bedroom, as you can see, has a large walk-in closet. And I love this." She took them into the master bathroom. "A marble tub with a built-in spa."

Susan loved the newness of the place. She could smell the wood of the cabinets and the rubbery carpet padding.

Jonathan said, "It's beautiful. I could use the other bedrooms for a den and a guest room—for when my great-granddaughters want to spend the weekend."

"Let me show you the others for comparison."

The other two places in the neighborhood were laid out identically. One was located on a corner lot, making it the most appealing of the three.

"I'm impressed," said Jonathan. I'd like to see a few more places to be sure, but I could be happy in La Puebla."

They got back into Blair's car. After a few minutes, she said, "I just thought of another place I'd like you to see. It's on the way back. It's a larger place in an older neighborhood, and it just went on the market."

Susan and Jonathan discussed the houses they'd just seen. Jonathan said he could envision being quite comfortable in any of the three. Blair pointed out plans to construct a park in the La Puebla community, complete with a swimming pool.

"Here we are," said Blair. She turned into an older neighborhood with larger homes and bigger yards.

Susan recognized the neighborhood. "This is where Matthew Chadwick lives. I was just here this morning. His place is beautiful, but I'm sure it cost him a pretty penny."

"There's always room for negotiation," said Blair.

"It's a completely different layout than the ones we just saw, and it has a lovely deck outside the kitchen door." She parked in the circular driveway.

Jonathan and Susan followed Blair into the fieldstone house. Susan's nose twitched. It may have just come on the market, but it smelled like it'd been boarded up for a while. Inside, it was as cold as it was outside.

"The kitchen is huge. I love the island which connects it to the dining room," said Blair.

After taking the tour, they wound up outside on the deck. Blair pointed across the yard. "That's the Chadwick house, and next to it lives a lovely couple with a teenage son. I know them from church. They just got back from an extended trip to Europe. Their son started college this fall, and they wanted to celebrate their newly empty nest, although I'm not sure how empty it really is. I hear their son comes home nearly every weekend since the college is close by."

"So they weren't in town the night Melissa Chadwick got killed, right?"

"What do you mean?" Blair seemed taken aback. Then she winked at Susan. Susan realized Blair didn't want to disclose to a potential buyer that one of the neighbors was recently murdered.

"It's okay. Jonathan knows all about it. I'll bet the murder has driven down the price." Susan digested what Blair just said. *Their son comes home nearly every weekend. Could he have been home the night of the murder?*

Jonathan spoke up. "Honestly, this place is way too big for one person. The places at La Puebla are more suitable."

"Let's head back to my office. I'll go through the listings tonight and see if there are others worth seeing tomorrow."

Chapter 15

Susan and Mike hung Mylar balloons over the dining room table and plastered a *Happy Birthday* banner on the wall. It was hard to believe Jonathan had been in town a week already.

"I wonder what's keeping Lynette. She was planning on coming over early to help me set up."

"She must be tied up at work. We'll hear from her soon. Shouldn't Jonathan be back by now?"

"Blair Cunningham was wonderful. When I told her we were planning a surprise party, she promised to keep Jonathan out house hunting until dinner time."

Susan spread out the birthday tablecloth and stacked plates and utensils. She couldn't wait for both Jonathan and Annalise to see the decorations. As she carried the punch bowl to the table, she heard her phone. Mike picked it up.

"Hey, Lynette. Okay, we're almost done decorating. See you soon." Mike relayed the message to Susan. "She and Jackson are finishing up with some new evidence, whatever that means."

"I'll bet it has to do with Melissa's murder."

"No crime talk tonight, promise? We're getting together to celebrate Jonathan's birthday, so let's stay away from talking about murder."

"Okay. You're right." She stepped back and admired the decorations. "I think we're done."

"It looks great. Let's sit down and catch our breaths before our guests arrive."

Mike clicked the remote and turned on the news.

Susan joined him on the couch. She was about to slouch into the sofa when she suddenly sat upright.

"Mike, look. Breaking news. Turn it up."

The reporter was standing in the woods in front of an evidence marker. "Late this afternoon, a hiker discovered the purse of murder victim Melissa Chadwick, assistant principal of Westbrook Charter School, and wife of Agrowmex's CEO, Matthew Chadwick, in the woods off Waffle Hollow Road."

"Mike, that must be the evidence Lynette was talking about! I'll bet the murderer threw it out of the car on the way to dump her body. Maybe they'll find fingerprints."

The doorbell rang. Janet, Susan's friend from the high school media center, stood there cradling a brightly wrapped box, topped with a bow. Janet was older than Susan but hadn't yet retired. Her husband had died several years ago, and she'd admitted to Susan she'd rather be busy and around people rather than alone in her big, empty house. Her son was in the military and rarely got home.

"Janet, you look great. Red is really your color."

"Thanks, Susan." She set the present on the coffee table. "I feel a bit out of place. I haven't met your father, and everyone else will be family."

"That isn't true. Theresa and Jackson are coming. The more, the merrier. Besides, I want Jonathan to start meeting people now that he'll be moving here." *I bet they'll hit it off. Janet is quiet, smart, and loves to travel, just like Jonathan.*

Theresa and Jackson arrived minutes before Lynette and Jason. Ian struggled to get down.

"He loves his newfound mobility," said Theresa. "Is it okay if I put him down?"

Susan nodded. "Look at that! This is the first time I've seen him walk. Good thing this house is well baby-proofed. Look at him go."

Annalise grabbed Mike's knees. "Hey, munchkin." He picked her up, pretending it was an effort. "You're getting bigger and prettier every time I see you."

Susan took Mia from Jason. "Come sit down. What can I get everyone to drink? I made my special punch."

Lynette followed Susan to the table to help. Out of Mike's earshot, Susan couldn't resist asking about the purse.

"I saw on the news that they found Melissa's purse. Anything pointing to a suspect?"

"Mom, we just started working on it. The murderer must have tossed it on his way from the Chadwicks' house to the bridge."

Susan's ears perked up. "So you think Melissa was killed at home? I thought you said there was no evidence of a crime scene there?" She was surprised Lynette let that slip.

"It'll be out in the news soon enough. A witness came forward who spotted a truck pulling into the Chadwick's driveway right after Melissa arrived home after the open house. He saw Melissa get into the truck with a man who was wearing a baseball cap. Of course, he couldn't give us much of a description."

"The witness—I'll bet it was the teenage son of the couple who was in Europe at the time of the murder. And the truck? It had to have been Larry Frisina's, the man who took over Melissa's job."

"He has an alibi. He was at Westbrook Elementary open house that night. And I'm not disclosing the name of the witness."

"He could have slipped out early. I'm sure Melissa did. Theresa saw her leaving from her classroom window." Her phone vibrated in her pocket. She handed Mia to Lynette. "It's a message from Blair Cunningham. She says she just finished with Jonathan, and he'll be here soon."

She returned to the living room. "Everybody hide! He's on the way." Susan flicked off the lights and worked her way to the floor behind the sofa. When she heard a knock, she grabbed the doorknob and said, "One, two, three… surprise."

Mike flipped on the lights. Susan's jaw dropped, and she heard Lynette gasp. Standing in the doorway—instead of Jonathan—were Audrey and Richard.

"Audrey? What are you doing here? You didn't tell me you and Richard were coming."

"It was on a whim. The temperature in Florida is still in the eighties. I wanted to spend Thanksgiving somewhere cold, with my daughter and her family."

Mike stepped forward and shook Richard's hand. "I hear congratulations are in order. We haven't seen you since you two tied the knot."

The door was still open when Jonathan arrived soon after. He looked back and forth between Audrey and Richard, shaking his head. "What are you doing here? Susan didn't tell me you were coming."

"I'm as surprised to see you as you are to see us."

Annalise yelled, "Surprise, GrampGramp!" She looked at Audrey, then turned to Richard, started screaming, and ran to Jason saying, "I'm scared of the monster. Pick me up."

Kids and animals can sense a person's soul. I don't see Ludwig or Johann in here either.

Mike said, "Come on in, everyone. Happy birthday, Jonathan."

Jonathan, looking bewildered over the sudden appearance of Audrey and his brother, scanned the room. "Is all this for me?"

"You only turn eighty once," said Susan. She realized she hadn't introduced her guests.

"Jonathan, Richard, and Audrey, this is Theresa and

Jackson Simpson, and Janet Flemming, the librarian from the school I normally volunteer at." *Did Jonathan just give Janet the once-over? He's smiling at her...* "Everyone, these are my birth parents, Audrey Roberts, um... Stirling, Jonathan Stirling and his brother, Richard Stirling. Richard is Audrey's husband." She swallowed hard. "Richard is my mother's husband and Jonathan's brother."

Jackson said, "So that makes him your uncle, right Susan."

"Technically, yes." It pained her to agree that Jackson was correct.

Sensing her uneasiness, Mike said, "Let's get this party started. Food is on the table. Grab a plate." He shooed the guests into the dining room. "Eat up. There's enough here to feed a small army."

Taking Mike's lead, the guests piled their plates high with pasta, salad, and garlic bread. Janet sat next to Jonathan to eat, and Susan noticed a lot of smiling and nodding between the two of them. After the ziti pan was nearly empty, Susan suggested opening presents.

Annalise clung to Jason's leg and avoided eye contact with Richard. Lynette and Jason gave Jonathan a gift certificate to Home Depot along with a colorful, homemade card courtesy of Annalise.

"You know I'll put this to good use," said Jonathan.

Next, he opened a large gift bag tied with ribbon. He pulled out a tweed coat from Susan and Mike. "Gloves too. Getting me ready for New York winters, huh?"

"This matches," said Theresa, handing Jonathan a brightly colored box. Jonathan unwrapped a cashmere scarf.

He rubbed the scarf on his cheek. "Soft as a whisper... thank you." He locked eyes with Janet. Susan could swear her father was blushing.

Janet said, "I made you a treat. Susan told me you

liked popcorn.”

“It's my favorite snack,” said Jonathan. He opened the box, which contained a tin full of popcorn drizzled with caramel and chocolate. “Did you make this yourself?”

“It's one of my specialties,” said Janet. She smiled and held her gaze on Jonathan long enough to indicate to Susan that she found him attractive.

Richard said, “We didn't know you'd be here.”

And if he did, would he have remembered his brother's birthday? Doubtful.

“This is beautiful. I'm so grateful to you all and touched that you put all this effort into making my birthday special. Do we have cake?”

“Of course we do. Can't celebrate a birthday without cake.” She headed to the kitchen, followed by Lynette. *One last splurge before I start Weight Watchers.*

“Mom, can you believe those two showed up like that?”

“Not at all. I'm sure Jonathan isn't happy to see Richard, though he's covering it well. He's such a gentleman.”

“Audrey doesn't seem like herself. She's awfully quiet and distant. She barely made a fuss over the girls. Remember when we went to Florida how she doted on Annalise? And this is the first time she's seen Mia.”

“Richard's probably sucked the energy right out of her. Let's get the cake on the table and hope Audrey and Richard don't overstay their welcome.”

“Are you supposed to be eating cake? It's full of sugar,” said Lynette.

Audrey entered the kitchen so quietly that Susan worried she'd heard what she'd said to Lynette. “Can I help you with anything?”

Lynette said, “There's a cake knife in the second drawer. Can you grab it?”

When Audrey reached for the knife, the sleeve of her sweater hiked up, and Susan noticed a purple bruise on her mother's wrist. "What happened there, Audrey?"

Audrey stammered. "I, um, I was lifting the groceries out of my trunk, and the carton of soda banged against it. You know how when you punch out the perforation in the carton so you can carry it? They're so poorly designed. I started to drop it, and I guess it left a bruise. Do you have candles?"

Lynette handed Audrey the candles and a lighter. "Why don't you bring these to the table, and I'll grab the cake."

When Audrey was out of earshot, Susan said, "Did you buy that story about the bruise being from the soda carton?"

"Not for a minute. I also noticed a deep scratch on her neck going toward her ear."

"Do you think Richard is hurting her?" The road between Susan and her birth mother had been rocky, but she certainly didn't wish her harm. She never liked Richard, especially now, seeing how he changed Audrey from a rational, strong, retired but still involved principal, into a starry-eyed fool. Susan wished she and Jonathan had refused to help back when Audrey insisted Richard was innocent of murdering his wife and begged them to get him out of jail.

"I think so," said Lynette. "I've seen my share of abuse victims as well as my share of liars, and Audrey fits the bill on both counts."

Mike called from the living room. "Let's get this party started. Annalise says she wants cake, and I have to agree with her."

Susan set the cake on the table, lit the candles, and turned out the lights. Janet, who had been standing next to Richard, inched her way around the table. As they sang, Susan again felt grateful that she'd found

Jonathan and Audrey but yearned for the mom and dad who raised her. She wondered what they'd think of Jonathan and Audrey if they were still alive. Would they all be friends? For a moment she imagined Jonathan blowing out the candles and her dad teasing him about not having enough air to do it in one breath. They'd both hate Richard; she was sure of that.

"Did you make a wish?" asked Jason.

"Don't have to. My wish already came true." In one enormous breath, Jonathan blew out every last candle.

Chapter 16

The next morning, Susan headed to Westbrook Charter. She couldn't believe Audrey and Richard had popped into Jonathan's surprise party uninvited last night. Richard was just plain gross. At the end of the evening, Janet confided in her that Richard whispered in her ear that she "was a ten" and they'd "make beautiful music together." *Yuck. Right in front of Audrey to boot.* She walked into Theresa's classroom, where Theresa and Satin were sorting homework copies.

"Hey, Susan. Great party last night," said Theresa. "Jonathan looked really happy."

"He was. What did you think of the surprise guests?"

"I thought it was weird that they just showed up without having called you to say they were coming to New York."

Satin said, "Who showed up?"

"My birth mother and her sleazy husband, who happens to be Jonathan's brother." Susan read Satin's expression. "It's complicated."

"I saw on the news that Melissa's purse was found. I wonder if the police have any new leads," said Satin.

"I think they're reconsidering the Chadwick's house as the initial crime scene. They didn't have any witnesses at first, but now they know the neighbor's teenage son was home. He says he saw a truck pull into the driveway the night Melissa was killed, and it was shortly after Melissa pulled into the garage."

Satin said, "What about Mr. Chadwick? Does he

have an alibi? It's always the husband."

"He wasn't in Mexico City, but he *was* out of town. I think he and Blair Cunningham bought themselves a little love nest in Puerto Vallarta."

After the kids left, Susan, Theresa, and Satin organized the donated school supplies and stuffed canvas bags for the foster kids. Satin had spearheaded a supply drive at the beginning of the school year, and her students had decorated the bags with fabric paint.

"What you're doing is touching," said Susan. "I hope the students learn from the example you're setting."

"People donate school supplies for the needy at the start of the school year, but kids go through crayons and pencils more quickly than they realize. I always reserve some to dole out later."

By the time they'd finished, it was late afternoon. Jonathan was out looking at houses again, and Susan offered to swing by the real estate office to pick him up. During the ride over, she tried to sort out what she knew about the murder.

Matthew has an alibi. Lynette said he was in Puerto Vallarta the night of the murder. Coincidentally, so was Blair Cunningham. Larry Frisina was at Westbrook Elementary's open house, but he could have slipped out early. He owns a blue truck, and the Chadwick's teenage neighbor saw a truck in their driveway the night Melissa was killed.

Melissa had some sort of proof that would threaten Larry Frisina and possibly his son, Chance. Matthew knows what Larry is hiding, but not where the proof is, or where it's hidden. He looked for it in Melissa's office. I suspect Jordan was looking for it also. Funny how quickly Melissa's son came to her office to pick up her things. And he doesn't have an alibi for the night his mother was killed. Chance has an alibi. He was working at ShopRite that night. Between Theresa, Jackson, and Lynette, Susan had pieced together that information.

She pulled into a space in front of the real estate office, but Blair and Jonathan hadn't yet returned. While waiting in the car, she continued her speculations.

Larry Frisina and Jordan have motives. Jordan doesn't have an alibi. Larry does, but he could have slipped out of the open house unnoticed. Then again, it may have nothing to do with either of them. Duncan Sitwell was forced to sell his land and has been vocal against Agrowmex. So has Della Hops and her cronies, but I think Della is harmless. Something is going on at Agrowmex. Mike and I heard a cow mooing, and since when did the craft fair sell veal? Susan watched as Blair parked behind her, and then accompanied her and Jonathan into Blair's office.

"Did you see anything good?" Blair hung up her coat and scarf.

Jonathan cleared his throat. "I've made a decision. I'm going to put a bid on the place in La Puebla. The one with the corner lot."

"Excellent choice," said Blair. "I'll start the ball rolling. I think you'll be very happy there."

Susan hugged her father. "It's really happening. You can be all moved in by Christmas."

Jonathan said, "My realtor in Atlanta says they have a date for the closing on my house. Christmas sounds about right. I dread the thought of packing my old place! I've accumulated lots of stuff over the years."

"It'll be worth it," said Susan. Jonathan smiled. "Let's go home, unless you need to sign anything."

"I'll get the paperwork ready, and he can come by in the morning," said Blair. "Congratulations on finding your new home."

Susan and Jonathan got into the Prius.

Jonathan said, "I have some news for you. You know the house in Puerto Vallarta? Blair says Matthew bought it to surprise his wife on their upcoming anniversary. She and Matthew aren't involved, I'm certain. She has a boyfriend. He called while we were house hunting. His name's Hector, and she spoke to him in Spanish on the phone."

Susan sighed. "Now it makes sense. The large withdrawal, the check on Blair's desk, the secret trip to Puerto Vallarta…"

"Where do we go from here?"

Susan loved that Jonathan enjoyed the amateur detective game.

"Either we find out what proof Melissa was hiding, or we explore the Agrowmex angle. Something more than growing produce is going on there, I feel it. And Duncan Sitwell may have killed Melissa to get back at Matthew for making him sell his place."

"Hmm. We passed Agrowmex on the way to my new home. We could turn around and see if we can do a bit of exploring." He looked at his watch. "They should be closed by now. Unless you're in a hurry to get home?"

"No. Mike won't be home for another hour, so I don't need to start dinner yet. Let's go for it."

Susan turned the car around and started for Agrowmex. It was just getting dark. Her phone vibrated, but she declined the call.

"Let me guess. Audrey?" said Jonathan.

"Yep. I hope she was calling to say good-bye before flying back to Florida."

"I doubt she'd be leaving so quickly. She's here for a reason. Maybe she'll confide in you before she leaves."

"She doesn't seem her usual, energetic self. I'm wondering how happy her marriage to Richard really is."

"I know my brother, and he's incapable of making anyone but himself happy."

They pulled into the Agrowmex parking lot, which was virtually empty. She and Mike had gone around the back the last time they came. "Let's take a walk. I have a flashlight on my phone." They walked toward the entrance.

She and Jonathan tried the front door of the factory, which was gated and locked. Then they walked around the back. "There's the fence Mike and I snuck through last time. That's where we heard the cow. Oh, and where we were shot at."

"Shot at?"

"Didn't I tell you about that? I'll fill you in later. We have to stay hidden."

They carefully stepped through the fence. Susan was surprised how agile Jonathan was. He was older but exponentially more limber. As they walked toward the rear entrance of the building, Susan heard the same mooing she'd heard last time. "See. I wasn't crazy!"

"Never said you were. I think it came from that direction." He did an about-face. "Follow me."

They took slow steps, checking to see if they were being watched. Susan cringed every time her foot landed on a noisy leaf. Then they heard the sound again.

"This way," said Jonathan. He led her toward the woods, which bordered the backside of the factory. When they got to the wall of trees, he said, "What's that?" He pointed to an opening in the trees.

Susan stuck her head through the opening. "It's a farmhouse. And a barn. I thought Agrowmex bought up all the land around the plant and leveled it. Why haven't they torn this one down? Let's go closer."

"It's a great hiding place. No one would have reason

to venture into these woods—except maybe us. Let's get a closer look. Watch your step."

Susan used her phone flashlight, but it was like trying to explore a cave using a candle. More than once, she tripped over roots before reaching their destination.

The tiny farmhouse was weathered, and bits of wood had fallen off the roof. Jonathan tugged at the door. "It's locked."

"Can you see in the window?" Susan rubbed dirt off the windowpane with her glove. "I don't see anyone." She rubbed another window clean. "There's a shotgun on the table!"

"Let's try the barn," said Jonathan. The wood was rotting in many places. He found a branch on the ground and, using it as leverage, pulled the lock right out of the door. A bat flew out and Susan screamed, ducking and covering her hair.

"I hope you had your rabies shot." Jonathan chuckled. "It's gone. I'll go in first." The light from his phone was dim, and the barn was clothed in darkness. They heard soft mooing but couldn't see where it was coming from.

"It smells putrid in here." Susan held her nose and struggled to see. "Hey, there's a cord hanging from the ceiling." One tug and the light bulb came to life.

"Oh my God," said Susan. "There are three baby cows in the stalls and blood on the ground. This is gross."

They carefully explored and saw an insulated door. When Jonathan pulled it open, a blast of cold air rushed out.

Susan screamed. "There's meat hanging from hooks. Is this what it looks like?"

Jonathan nodded. "I think we just found ourselves a small slaughterhouse."

"We have to call Lynette. The police have to see

this."

"Not so fast. They can't bust into private property without probable cause or a warrant."

Susan called 911. "Help! I heard shots fired behind Agrowmex. They came from a barn in the woods. Hurry!" She hung up before the operator could ask her name, then turned to Jonathan. "How's that for probable cause?"

Chapter 17

The next morning, Susan turned on the TV in her bedroom while she got ready. "Look, Mike. The police invaded the woods behind Agrowmex last night. Looks like one of those drug busts or a swat team. See. They're ripping open the barn door."

"Funny how they knew to go there."

"Lynette said someone made an anonymous call. Said they heard shots fired."

"And when the police got there, they found a secret slaughterhouse. Amazing. I've gotta get to work. See you at dinner." Mike gave her a kiss.

Susan added: "I may be late. I have a meeting with Matthew Chadwick this evening about setting up the scholarship."

When Susan arrived at school, the mailroom was buzzing with the news about Agrowmex.

"I'll bet they've already arrested Matthew Chadwick," said the secretary.

Theresa said, "I heard he knew nothing about it. A group of his employees secretly set it up and were keeping all the profits."

The chatter continued, cut short by the bell which signaled the day was about to begin.

Susan focused on helping Theresa's students make Thanksgiving placemats. She had never developed a love of arts and crafts, but helping the kids paint and glue satisfied her creative side. Maybe she and Annalise could make Christmas ornaments together. On second thought, baking and decorating cookies sounded more appealing. She reminded herself of the afternoon Weight Watchers meeting she'd vowed to attend. *I could wait until the new year.* Having procrastinated long enough, she pushed the thought aside. *It's now or never.*

"Susan, would you mind running downstairs and making more copies?" asked Theresa. "I thought I'd made enough turkey patterns, but I was wrong. Kids learn to read in kindergarten, but in fourth grade, they still can't cut a straight line."

"I'm on it," said Susan. She passed through the front office and stopped mid-step as she watched the secretary remove a painting from the wall behind her desk. She placed the painting on the floor and opened a small wall safe.

"A hidden safe. Who knew?" said Susan.

Stephanie said, "Overkill if you ask me. There's never more than a few dollars collected for field trips or class pictures stashed in here. That and a few papers Melissa and Dr. Russo tossed in there. See?"

She held up a manila envelope labeled with Melissa's name. "I don't know what I'm supposed to do with this."

Susan held out her hand. "I'm going to the Chadwicks' house later today to discuss the scholarship with Matthew. I can bring it to him."

The secretary handed it to her. "Thanks."

For the rest of the afternoon, Susan wondered what was inside the envelope. She knew opening it wasn't right, yet whatever was important enough for Melissa to stash in a safe, could be vital to solving her murder. She should open it for Melissa's sake. *What am I talking about? Tampering with mail was a federal offense, wasn't it?*

After school, Susan drove downtown to the Weight Watchers meeting, which was held in a back area of a bookstore. Distracted by the displays of new books, she was compelled to pick up a few, read the backs, and flip through the pages. She made a mental note of which ones to add to her Christmas wish list. In stark contrast to the cozy displays, she walked around the partition and was confronted with a cold, metallic scale. *This must be the true-crime section.* She shuddered.

The receptionist, a grandmotherly, gray-haired lady said, "Haven't seen you before. Are you a new member?"

"I'm signing up today."

"Welcome. You can pay weekly or sign up for a block. It's cheaper that way."

Susan was determined to stick with it and opted to pay for the block. After all, she'd hate to skip a meeting she'd already paid for. After the painful part was over, she stepped off the scale and sat down. About a dozen people, including a few men and a young woman rocking a baby carriage, sat in the metal folding chairs, studying the new materials or chatting with other members. She felt instantly at home, hearing others' struggles with eating, and at the same time she was inspired. One woman had lost over a hundred pounds. She walked out with recipes, strategies, and hope.

Once in the car, she looked at the manila envelope sitting on the passenger seat. *What harm would it do? I'll put it back when I'm done, and no one will be the wiser.* She carefully unclasped the envelope and pulled out the contents.

No way. This is a private investigator's report. She read through it twice. In summary, it said that Jordan Chadwick was selling drugs to Chance Frisina. There were even snapshots included, which looked like they'd been shot with a long-range camera, like the ones she'd seen private investigators use on TV. *This has to be the proof Matthew and Jordan were looking for. And if it was made public, Chance would be implicated as well.*

Then she pulled out another photo. This one had a white border and crease lines running through it.

It's a picture of two young children. A boy and a girl, both in overalls. I thought Jordan was their only child. The children resembled each other, but their coloring was completely different than Jordan's. *Maybe Melissa's their aunt or a godmother.*

Susan put everything back into the envelope and drove to Matthew Chadwick's. As soon as she pulled into the development, she was blinded by bright lights. Police cars and reporters crowded around Matthew's house. She parked down the road. "Excuse me, what's happening here?"

A reporter pointed to the house. It was spray-painted with the message *Go to jail, murderer!,* and plush toy cows littered the front stoop.

"Do they know who did this?"

The reporter answered, "Not for sure, but it has to be one of the animal rights groups."

Della Hops? She called Matthew Chadwick from the car to see if he wanted to postpone their meeting. They rescheduled for the next day, and Susan turned the car around.

"Jonathan, Mike, I'm home." Susan was surprised that neither Mike nor Jonathan were in the living room. *Mike's car is in the driveway. Did they go for a walk?* She checked upstairs. "Mike. Jonathan."

When she came back downstairs, she heard the sliding glass door open.

"Surprise," said Mike. "Jonathan and I decided to grill a steak before we cover up the barbecue for the winter. I threw a few potatoes in the oven. They should be about done."

"It's freezing out." She took the platter from Mike. "But what a great idea. I have to look up the points for steak and baked potato, then I'll be right there." She flipped through the points booklet she'd received at the meeting. *Points are just calories in sheep's clothing.*

Mike said, "How was your meeting with Matthew Chadwick?"

"Haven't you seen the evening news? Someone spray-painted graffiti all over his house. We postponed the meeting. Judging by the message, looks like an animal rights activist did it."

Jonathan said, "In retaliation for the slaughterhouse, no doubt."

"I spoke to Lynette. She says Matthew denies knowing it was on the grounds."

"Someone was running that little side business. Hard to believe they were doing it right under his nose," said Susan.

The doorbell rang, and Susan started to stand up.

"I'll get it," said Jonathan. "Eat your steak before it gets cold."

"When I talked to Lynette, she wanted to know what time they should come over for Thanksgiving," said Mike. "I said I'd check with you."

"The holidays are sneaking up on me this year. I hadn't thought about it yet." She heard Audrey's voice. Jonathan escorted her and Richard into the dining room.

Audrey carried a bakery box. "We can't cook in our hotel, so when we walked by the bakery earlier, I picked up this pumpkin cheesecake. Can't show up for Thanksgiving dinner empty-handed now. I can't believe it's the day after tomorrow."

Richard said, "Audrey wanted to buy a plain old pumpkin pie. She's not the most imaginative woman I've ever met. Come to think of it, not the most imaginative woman or man I've ever met. I said we needed something special for our first Thanksgiving together as a family." He gave Jonathan a slap on the back. Susan looked into Jonathan's eyes and read his thoughts.

"I thought you'd be gone before the holiday," said Susan. She emphasized the word *gone,* although she hadn't forgotten Audrey telling her she wanted to spend the holiday with *family.*

"We're going to stay and celebrate together, remember? Thanksgiving in shorts and sandals doesn't cut it. All the years I've lived in Florida, I still can't get used to it."

"Audrey's just self-conscious about exposing her cellulite-laden thunder thighs in summer clothing. Right, Audrey?"

Susan pitied her. When she'd first met Audrey, she was strong and confident. Now she sat there while her husband insulted her over and over again. Even her body language had changed to reflect her insecurities.

Mike started a pot of coffee. "Let's go sit in the living room. Susan, don't we have a pound cake in the freezer?"

Great. I started Weight Watchers hours ago and don't need the temptation of pound cake.

"Yeah, it's here. And we have ice cream too." Mike put the cake in the microwave and carried plates into the living room. "I wonder if there's any more news on the slaughterhouse." He grabbed the remote and turned on the news. "Isn't that the music teacher from your old school?"

"Yes, Duncan Sitwell. He replaced me when I retired. He's quite vocal about his opposition to the new charter school but comes by to give after-school guitar lessons a few days a week. Such a hypocrite. What's he doing on the news?"

Mike turned up the volume. "He's giving some sort of speech. He's starting a petition to run Agrowmex out of town. Wow, he sounds hateful talking about

Matthew Chadwick."

"Guess he doesn't believe Mr. Chadwick was blind to the slaughterhouse operation," said Jonathan.

"Just another nail in the coffin he wishes contained dead Mexicans and other job-stealing immigrants," said Susan.

Richard reached for a second piece of cake. "What's wrong with making a little money on the side? He owned the land. I say let the man run whatever business he wants. Bleeding-heart animal rights people. Ugh."

Audrey reached for another piece of cake. Richard slapped her hand. "Now, Audrey. One piece is enough. You're getting a little pudgy around the middle since our wedding. If you don't keep that girlish figure, don't blame me if my eyes stray."

"If Audrey wants more cake, she can have it. Pudgy my foot. Here." Susan cut a piece for Audrey.

"No, he's right. I don't need it."

"We should be going anyway. I want to be back to the hotel in time to catch the football game. Come on, Audrey. We'll see everyone on Thanksgiving."

After they left, Susan ranted about Richard's treatment of Audrey. "Audrey looks beaten down. When I first met her, no way she'd stand for that treatment. Pudgy? What a complete jerk."

"We'll get through Thanksgiving and hopefully won't see them again anytime soon. Don't let them ruin our holiday," said Mike.

"I won't." She'd resisted the pound cake up until now, but thinking about sharing the holiday with Richard and Audrey ruined her resolve. She ate two pieces before going to bed.

Chapter 18

The next morning, Susan and Mike sat down to breakfast. Despite the pound cake detour, Susan's blood sugar was down this morning. Using her Weight Watchers booklet, she calculated the points for a scrambled egg, a slice of whole-wheat toast, and the milk she used in her coffee. Then she opened a can of Fancy Feast for Ludwig and Johann. She wished she'd never started buying wet cat food. Now it was all they'd eat. Both cats came running as soon as she popped the top open.

Mike read the paper. "Look, here's an article about the Agrowmex incident. Matthew Chadwick is quoted saying he knew nothing about the slaughterhouse and will cooperate with the police to find out who was responsible. He says he will salvage the company's good name and someday pass it on to his son, Jordan."

"Does it say anything about the vandalism to his house?"

"Just that it happened and the police are looking for leads. Are you still going over there this morning?"

"Yes. We have to finalize the details of the memorial scholarship. Shouldn't take long. I'll be back in time to pick up Evan at the airport. I'm so excited to see him."

"I'm glad his orthopedics rotation doesn't call for weekends. Some of his friends are stuck in St. Louis. Do we have everything we need for tomorrow?"

"The turkey is defrosted. I'll put together the stuffing tonight. Tomorrow we just have to throw together the green bean casserole and bake the rolls. Lynette's bringing everything else—except dessert. We have the pumpkin cheesecake Audrey and Richard brought over."

Jonathan walked into the kitchen and poured himself a cup of coffee. "And I'll pick up a bottle of wine. I can't wait to meet Evan. You must be so proud of him."

"We are," said Susan. "I'm sure the two of you will hit it off."

She put clean sheets on Evan's bed and fresh towels in the bathroom before leaving. She hoped the meeting would be quick. The day before Thanksgiving it was hard to focus on business. She'd rather stay home and watch Martha Stewart guest-appearing on the morning shows, demonstrating how to fold napkins into turkeys.

The sky was dreary with the clouds stiflingly low over the mountains. Snow was predicted for later in the evening. She hoped they'd be back from the airport by then. When she pulled into Matthew's neighborhood, she saw his car in the driveway and wondered why he hadn't parked it in their double garage. *I wish we had a garage. I hate getting into a freezing cold car. I hate it even more when I have to scrape ice off the windshield.*

The graffiti hadn't yet been removed from Matthew's home. The ugly black-and-red message across the front of the house made it look like burnt toast amidst a tray of Christmas cookies. Several houses in the upper-class neighborhood already sported wreaths and colorful lights.

She rang Matthew's doorbell twice, but no one answered. She turned the doorknob and was surprised the front door wasn't locked.

"Matthew, it's me, Susan! We had a meeting scheduled this morning—are you here?"

She tried calling his name again, then ventured through the foyer and into the living room. Matthew was lying on the floor by the fireplace. "Matthew, are you okay?"

As she got closer, she realized he was far from okay. He was lying face down with a bloody gash on the back of his head. She shook inside. *Not another murder. He can't be dead!*

She bent down and felt for a pulse, but even before she touched his cold neck and listened for breathing, she already knew he was dead. A bloody fireplace poker was next to the body. Trembling, Susan called 911, then paced around the living room. Then she panicked. *What if the murderer is still in the house?* She ran outside, closed the door, and sat on the front stoop.

Ow, what am I sitting on? She got up and noticed speckled beads on the stoop and in the adjacent flower bed. Then she bent down and picked up a piece of string. *This looks like a broken bracelet. I wonder if it was Melissa's. No, the police or Matthew would have seen it before now.* She sat on the stoop, jumping up and waving when she heard sirens.

"He's in here. I found him dead on the floor, and there's a murder weapon next to him. A fireplace poker. And it has blood on it. His head too. He's got a bloody gash on his head."

Although this wasn't the first murder victim she'd ever discovered, it didn't get easier. She felt sick to her stomach, looking at the lifeless body sprawled across the Mexican floor tiles. Within minutes, Lynette and Jackson arrived.

"Mom, what happened? Are you okay? Did you see who did this? You could have been killed yourself. How is it you always get in the middle of these things?"

Lynette, I…" She told Lynette step by step what had happened. "Do you think it has to do with the slaughterhouse? Either someone was angry—like the person who spray-painted the house, or someone wanted to make sure Matthew wasn't able to help find the true culprits."

"Mom, it's too early to speculate. Are you sure you're okay? Aren't you supposed to pick up Evan today? Go home. I'll get an officer to drive you. There's nothing to do here. It'll be hours before we know anything."

"I can drive myself." Reluctantly, Susan got back into her car. *Poor Jordan. Both his parents murdered in such a short time period. And with the holidays coming up—even more horrible. Unless* he *killed his parents. Melissa had a private investigator's report proving he was dealing drugs. He had an argument with his mother the day she was killed and one with his father before the memorial service. Now, with his father dead, Jordan inherits the company.*

She had a hard time believing a child could murder his parents, although since getting to know her birth mother, Audrey, the thought had crossed her mind once or twice. She tried to stop picturing the scene she'd just walked in on, but she couldn't get it out of her mind. She was so preoccupied she nearly ran a stop sign on the way home.

"Susan, is that you?" Mike called to her from the kitchen. She smelled herbs and cooked celery. "I'm getting the stuffing ready for tomorrow."

Head down, body drooping, she walked into the kitchen.

"Susan, what's wrong? Didn't the meeting go well?"

"Mike, you're never going to believe this. When I got to Matthew's house, he was lying dead on the living room floor. A bloody fireplace poker was next to him. I walked right into a crime scene."

"Not again! I mean, are you okay? It must have been horrible. Matthew Chadwick is dead?"

"Yes, first Melissa is murdered and now Matthew.

Lynette sent me home. They're processing the crime scene. It was awful, finding him like a mannequin toppled over on the floor of his own living room."

"Do they have any suspects?"

Jonathan walked in. "Suspects for what? Susan, what's wrong?"

Susan explained what had happened, tensing as she again relived the scene. "I don't know. Maybe it's related to the slaughterhouse discovery. Maybe his son Jordan…"

"Susan, you can't speculate. Lynette will find the son of a bee. Come on, try to take a nap before we go pick up our son."

"I won't be able to sleep. I can't stop picturing what I saw."

"Then help me finish the stuffing and try to relax. You don't want Evan to see you upset. You know how he worries about you."

Jonathan said, "Didn't Blair Cunningham call this a safe little town? I felt safer back in Atlanta. I'm sorry you had to be the one to find him. If you or Lynette need help, I'm here."

Mike gave him a look. "She doesn't need help because she's going to leave the investigation up to the professionals. There's a psychopath murderer out there. What do you think he'll do if he realizes the two of you are on his tail?"

"You're absolutely right. Besides, Susan has to help me decorate and settle into my new home. I'm flying to Atlanta the day after Thanksgiving to pack up my place, and after the closing on my new home, I'll need plenty of help."

"It's almost time to leave for the airport. Traffic's going to be terrible with it being the busiest travel day of the year. Let's go get our son."

Chapter 19

During the trip to the airport, Susan tried to push the murder out of her brain and focus on seeing her son, but it was difficult. The horrible image, her self-made list of potential suspects—it was like telling someone not to think of elephants.

"I see a Delta flight coming in for a landing. I'll bet Evan's on it." Mike turned into the parking garage.

"I can't wait to see him. We'll have to take him with us to pick out a Christmas tree this weekend. Jonathan and the girls can help us decorate." She felt better thinking about spending the holidays together and with the new additions—Mia and Jonathan.

Susan could spot her son a mile away. He was wearing a green *Wash U* sweatshirt, carrying a leather backpack over one shoulder and pushing a carry-on next to him. Fidgeting, she waited as he came closer to her arms.

"Evan, how was your flight? Did they feed you?" She hugged him tightly. Now her heart felt whole—at least until he had to leave again.

"It was fine, Mom. Crowded, but I managed to sleep most of the way. Dad, you look great."

"Mom and I are back to walking after dinner. Been running?"

"It's tough with my schedule. I play volleyball and basketball whenever I can. That keeps me in shape."

On the way home, Susan caught up with the ins and outs of Evan's orthopedic rotation, which he freely shared. He was tight-lipped, however, about his dating life. He wouldn't even tell her the name of the girl he'd been seeing. A light snow fell on the windshield, but the Wiles family was safely at home before the real storm started.

"I told you Jonathan is moving here, right? He found a cute little place near Agrowmex. He's flying to Atlanta day after tomorrow to pack up his house and should be back here by Christmas."

"I'll be back home for Christmas. I can help him move into the new place."

Mike grabbed Evan's suitcase and followed Susan to the door. "Ludwig and Johann will be thrilled to see you. I think they knew you were coming. They watched optimistically as I changed your sheets and made up your bed."

As predicted, both cats greeted them at the door. Johann immediately began rubbing against Evan's leg while Ludwig looked up at him and meowed. Jonathan was waiting in the living room.

"I'm assuming you're Evan," said Jonathan. "You look just like your father."

Evan shook his hand. "Nice to finally meet you. I heard you're moving here. Mom's really excited about that."

"Speaking of family," said Jonathan. The doorbell rang as if on cue. "Audrey called earlier. I let it slip that Evan was flying in, and she said she'd stop by to see him."

Susan rolled her eyes and opened the door. Audrey rushed in, followed by her ex-con hubby, Richard.

"Evan, I've missed you," said Audrey. She gave him a squeeze. "My rheumatologist and I were talking about you. He said Banyan Beach is the place to be if you're thinking of doing an orthopedic residency. His friend does hip replacements all day long, one after another, and he lives in one of those million-dollar condos on the beach." She brushed snow off her coat. "And you can't beat the weather in Florida."

"Especially if you're one of the old folks. Right, Audrey?" Richard turned to Evan. "Your grandmother's so brittle she'd shatter if she fell on a stack of mattresses. Right, Audrey?"

Susan stepped between Audrey and Richard. "She's still instrumental in running a school and looks half her age," said Susan. "Hope when I get old I'm doing as well as she is."

"You *are* old," said Mike. Susan gave him a swat. "I meant wise. Young as a spring chicken with the mind of a sage." She swatted him again before taking everyone's coat.

Mike started the coffee. "How about we order Chinese? Audrey and Richard, will you be joining us?"

Susan telepathically glared at him from the living room.

"We'd love to stay and catch up with Evan," said Audrey. She and Richard sat on opposite ends of the sofa with Evan, Ludwig, and Johann between them.

Susan couldn't resist. "Evan tells me the very best residency programs are right here in the Northeast. Columbia and NYU are a stone's throw away." Her phone rang. "It's Lynette. I'll be right back."

She took the call in the kitchen. "Lynette, we just got back from the airport and Audrey…"

"Mom, I'd love to catch up, but first I have to ask you something. When I got back to the station after leaving the Chadwick's house, I had a phone message waiting. It was from Matthew."

"Really? What did it say?"

"He said he knew who killed Melissa and asked if he could come by after he met with you about the scholarship."

"Then he was murdered sometime between the

phone call and when I found him."

"Yes. Did you see anything unusual when you arrived at his house, or did he say anything to you previously that hinted at who he was talking about?"

"Not that I can remember, but the graffiti happened last night. Do you suppose it's related?"

"It wasn't Della Hops. She and her gang were selling crocheted Christmas ornaments at the twenty-four-hour indoor flea market. We have witnesses. It amazes me people were out shopping at that hour."

"Was she there at the time Matthew's house was spray-painted."

"Yes. It wasn't her. And her band of cohorts was with her all night too, crocheting personalized ornaments on the spot."

Susan imagined Della's thug-like cronies crocheting Christmas ornaments behind a table at the flea market and shuddered. "I'll try to remember if I saw or heard anything. I do remember that the door was unlocked. He told me once that the front door was never unlocked, but he found it that way the night Melissa was killed."

"Okay. We'll see you tomorrow. I made my squash casserole, and I'll bake a batch of biscuits in the morning. Tell Evan I said hi."

Mike was pouring coffee when Susan accidentally bumped into him. The coffee splattered on his hand and shirt.

"Ow. Watch where you're going, lady. I'm going to have coffee stains on my twenty-year-old *Jets* jersey."

Susan looked at his hand. "I'm so sorry. Let me grab a washcloth. Meanwhile, run your hand under cool water."

She climbed the steps to retrieve the washcloth and heard Richard whispering on the phone in the guest room.

"Yeah, it's going according to plan. Perfect cover. It'll be there in two days." Richard slipped down the stairs without realizing that Susan had overheard the conversation. She grabbed a washcloth and slipped back into the kitchen.

Chapter 20

Susan and Mike awoke at the crack of dawn to get the food started.

"I smell turkey," said Evan. He stuck his head in the fridge, then opened every cabinet looking for breakfast options. "Dad, how about some of your famous French toast?"

"I'm a little busy at the moment. If you want to help me peel and mash these potatoes first…"

"Never mind. I found a box of Cheerios. Are these expired?"

Susan turned off the vacuum and walked in just in time to answer. "Cheerios don't expire." She pulled a bowl out of the dishwasher. "And I guarantee the milk is fresh."

"What time is everyone coming over? I can't wait to see Annalise. We *FaceTime* each other, isn't that cool? She knows how to do it all by herself without Lynette helping her."

"She's a genius," said Mike.

Susan poured herself a cup of coffee. "Wait till you see Mia. She'll be walking any minute." She sat down at the table with the tome of a newspaper and separated the ads according to proximity and percentage of discount. Mapping out Black Friday shopping was a favorite tradition, and, luckily, Lynette was off tomorrow so they could go together.

"Anyone up for a morning walk?" asked Jonathan. He entered the dining room wearing sweats, a knitted cap, and a puffer vest.

"Evan used to have a vest just like that," said Susan.

"I found it in the closet. Felt like I might need another layer. Who's coming with me?"

Mike was peeling potatoes, and Evan was still eating breakfast.

"I'll come along," said Susan. "I have a little time before I start cooking."

She got herself together and went out with Jonathan, hoping to mull over details of the now double murder case. In spite of the gloomy weather forecast, the sun was bright and she wished she'd brought along her sunglasses.

Jonathan said, "What do we know about Matthew Chadwick's murder? I'm assuming it's related to his wife's death. Who wanted both of them dead?"

"He left a message for Lynette saying he knew who killed his wife. Whoever killed her must have known Matthew was on to him."

"Someone wanted both of them dead. That eliminates Melissa's school enemies, if she had any. They'd have had no reason to go after Matthew."

"Unless Matthew was a threat because he figured out who killed Melissa."

"What about the son? Who gets the business now that Matthew's dead?"

"Jordan's their only child, so I suppose it's him. He argued with Melissa the night she died. Maybe he was arguing with his father over the same thing."

They walked to the end of the street and turned around. Susan was having moderate success following her new food plan and bringing her blood sugar under control. If she could make it through the holidays, she knew she could get into a routine once the new year started.

"Did they find out who was responsible for the amateur slaughterhouse?"

"Not yet, but Lynette was convinced it was happening under Matthew's nose. She couldn't see him being sidetracked like that. Besides, Agrowmex was doing well on its own."

When they got back to the house, the golden brown turkey was cooling on the counter, and Susan put the pan of stuffing in the oven. Lynette arrived a little while later with a squash casserole and biscuits. Evan played with Annalise and Mia, while Jason brought in folding chairs. Audrey and Richard arrived just as the food was being set out on the table.

"I smell a feast," said Richard. "When Audrey attempts to cook, our place smells like the Everglades are on fire."

Audrey looked at the floor. Sensing her unease, Evan said, "I love grandma's cooking. When I was in Florida, she made me the best pasta carbonara I'd ever tasted."

On the way to the table, Lynette's phone dinged, and she pulled it out of her pocket to read a text. Susan tried to read over her shoulder, but Lynette swatted her away. She whispered to Lynette. "Any murder news?"

"Mom…"

"I'm directly involved. I found Matthew's body, and I won't feel safe while his murderer is out there."

"No, but they picked up the two guys responsible for operating the amateur meat business. One was an employee, the other did sporadic maintenance work for the company. They both swear Matthew Chadwick knew nothing about it. The employee bragged about how easy it was to pull the wool over Chadwick's eyes. Oh, and one of them owns a shotgun."

With Mia strapped into a high chair and Annalise next to Mike on a booster seat, Thanksgiving dinner officially began. Lynette and Susan had Jonathan's new house fully furnished by the end of the meal, with

Susan promising to take him to her favorite furniture store when he returned from Atlanta.

"I was thinking about moving back here myself," said Richard. Audrey glared at him from across the table.

Jonathan said, "You did spend thirty-plus years up here, mostly while you were incarcerated."

Richard ignored the comment. "I'm not crazy about the Florida weather. And I sense some business opportunities here."

"Florida is my home," said Audrey. "And even though I'm officially retired, I'll always hold Hemingway High dear to my heart."

"How about some pie?" suggested Mike. "And I can't wait to cut into that pumpkin cheesecake you brought over the other day, Audrey."

Susan began stacking the dirty dishes.

"Sit down, Susan. Richard and I will get these."

Mia squirmed in her high chair. "I think someone needs a diaper change," said Jason.

While Jason tended to Mia, Lynette freed Annalise from the booster seat and followed her into the living room. Evan tailed behind them. Susan found herself alone at the table, able to relax for a few moments. Richard's phone, which he'd left behind, lit up with a text message. Susan read it to herself. *On time. Will pick up.* She couldn't imagine what Richard could be expecting here in New York. After all, he'd be back in Florida in a day or two.

"Here we go," said Mike. "Pumpkin cheesecake, apple pie, and pumpkin pie. Lynette, Evan, come on in. Dessert time."

Susan saw Richard check his phone on his lap.

"We need to be going. Come on, Audrey."

"Going where?" said Audrey. "We haven't had dessert yet."

"I'm suddenly not feeling well. Besides, you don't need any calorie-laden dessert."

"Richard, why don't you go, and we'll drop Audrey off on her way home," said Lynette.

"Well… okay. But not too late. She needs her beauty sleep."

After Richard left, the mood was more relaxed. Audrey was less tense and chatted freely before playing tea party with Annalise in the living room. Stuffed and happy, Susan solidified her Black Friday plans with Lynette.

"Don't forget, we're going to the tree lot tomorrow afternoon," said Evan. "We can pick you up too, Audrey."

"I don't know. Richard isn't much for Christmas trees."

"He wasn't invited. Think about it," said Susan.

Mia was getting cranky. "We're going to go before she has a tantrum," said Lynette. "I'll talk to you in the morning."

Chapter 21

Black Friday shopping and yesterday's festivities required a restorative nap. Waking up refreshed, Susan cleared a spot in the living room for the Christmas tree they were about to buy.

"Mike, did you get the ornaments out of the attic? Did you find the outdoor lights?"

"Done," said Mike. He set a large Tupperware container full of ornaments on the couch. "Evan said he'd help with the outdoor lights over the weekend."

Susan, Evan, and Mike were lucky to find a parking place at the crowded Christmas tree lot. They made their way down the first aisle. Trying to remember the virtues of a Douglas fir over a Fraser fir, Susan almost ran directly into Satin and her boyfriend, Trey.

"Susan! How was your Thanksgiving?"

"Lovely, Satin. And yours?"

"Extra special this year. I was finally cleared to be a foster parent. Trey and I spent yesterday at child services, serving up turkey and all the trimmings. Then we ate with the cutest set of twins you ever saw. Brother and sister, eight years old. Mom's dead and the father's in jail. It's hard to get a family to take on two at once. Can you imagine how hard it is being separated from your sibling, especially when all you have is each other?"

"Never gave it much thought, but I can see how hard it would be."

Satin nodded at Susan and continued. "I've decided those twins were destined to be with me. We're picking them up later today for a visit. You'll have to come to our tree-trimming party tonight and meet them."

"What tree-trimming party?" said Trey.

"Well, I just came up with it. Sudden inspiration. I'm going to call Theresa. Hopefully they'll be available. This town needs some cheerfulness what with two back-to-back murders."

Trey said, "Isn't your daughter a detective? Do they have any leads?"

"Not yet."

"A woman gets thrown off a railroad bridge and then her husband is bludgeoned to death with a fireplace poker. There has to be a clue in there somewhere. I'll bet it's the son. I heard he's into some shady dealings," said Trey.

"Enough talk about murder. Can I count you in for tonight?"

"Sounds like fun," said Evan. Susan realized she hadn't officially introduced Evan to them.

"Your mom is so happy you're home. She talks about you all the time," said Satin. "That's the kind of love a child deserves. Well, back to tree shopping, or there won't be a party. See you at seven."

Susan and Evan caught up with Mike, who'd gone ahead, scouting acceptable tree choices.

"What do you think about this one?" He pulled on the branches and said, "It's fresh and symmetrical too."

"Definitely an option," said Susan. "Let's keep looking to make sure."

They continued their quest, eliminating trees that were too small, too tall, too scraggly, too brown, or too lopsided.

"The one I found is looking better and better," said Mike.

"I'm convinced," said Susan. They turned around and headed back to the other tree. "Hey, there's Larry

Frisina."

"Mrs. Wiles, hope you're enjoying your time off."

"Very much. This is my husband Mike and my son Evan."

"Nice to meet you. My son is around the corner. Hey, Chance, come here. I want you to meet someone."

Chance sauntered around the corner. He was thinner than he'd been in the picture in Larry's office.

"How's it going?" Chance shook their hands. "Dad, let's pick one and get home."

"Okay. We're leaving now. See you Monday, Mrs. Wiles."

Mike and Evan grabbed the tree and brought it to the cashier.

Evan said, "What's with that boy, Chance? He looks like a drug addict."

"He was, but he went to rehab, and word is he's doing well. If he was still having trouble, rumors would be flying at work."

"Once an addict, always an addict. Did you notice how sweaty his hands were?"

"He could be right," said Mike. "It's forty degrees out, and his hair was damp on his forehead."

"Maybe he's got a fever. Anyway, let's get home and set this baby up."

Getting the tree home was infinitely easier with Evan's help. Between the three of them, the lights and ornaments were in place in record time. Susan snapped a photo to send to Lynette and Jonathan. She figured Jonathan would be home by now. Next year they'd help him set up a tree in his new house. Hey, it was possible he'd be settled in time to put one up this year. The closing was scheduled for the week before Christmas. She high-fived Mike and Evan.

"Done. More beautiful than ever. Can't wait for Annalise and Mia to see it. I almost forgot..." She ran upstairs to retrieve an ornament wrapped in tissue paper. "I picked this up weeks ago. It says *Baby's First Christmas*. I had them paint Mia's name on it. The year too."

"Shouldn't that be hanging on their own tree?" said Mike.

"Don't worry. I bought two. Gave the other to Lynette this morning when we went shopping."

"There's more of that pumpkin cheesecake left, right?"

"Yes, plenty. I'll make some hot chocolate."

All three curled up in the living room with their snacks and Netflix. Thanks to Evan, they were hooked on the BBC series, *Sherlock*. After binge watching back-to-back episodes, Susan pulled out leftover turkey and squash casserole for a quick dinner before heading to Satin's. They parked behind Theresa's car, and knocked on the door.

"Susan, Mike, Evan—how'd your own tree trimming go?" Satin wore a Christmas sweater and black leggings.

"Up and running," said Mike. "Many hands make light work."

"Are you ready for round two?" said Trey. "Theresa and Jackson are inside."

"And I want you to meet our special guests," said Satin. They followed her into the living room. "This is Gabby and her brother Daniel."

"Pleased to meet you," said Susan.

Mike reached out his hand to shake. Daniel stepped forward, but Gabby hid behind Satin. Susan thought Gabby was like a much younger child but attributed her insecurity to lack of a stable home life.

"This is a friend, Gabby. She volunteers at my school. You don't have to be scared."

Gabby clung to Satin's waist, and Susan thought it

best not to pressure her. "There's Jackson and Theresa. Excuse me."

Susan worked her way over to her friends, while Mike and Evan loaded their plates at the snack table. "Where's Ian?"

"We got a sitter. As much as I love him, chasing a toddler around an unfamiliar house complete with a tree in the living room, Christmas ornaments, and other enticing dangers isn't my idea of relaxing."

Susan remembered those days and wondered how she ever had the energy to deal with chasing toddlers and dealing with temper tantrums. Seeing Gabby and Daniel, she was reminded that each age had its challenges.

"I heard your father is moving to town," said Jackson. "Theresa says he already bought a house over by Agrowmex."

"Yes. He's packing up his place in Atlanta as we speak. After the two recent murders, I'm surprised he didn't have second thoughts. Any progress?"

"We narrowed down Matthew's time of death. He was murdered a few hours before you arrived. We think between six and ten in the morning."

"When I was at the Chadwicks' the first time, I saw an appointment on his calendar for that very day. I couldn't read his handwriting with any degree of certainty, but it may have been an eight I saw scribbled in the square of his desk calendar. I'll bet he had an eight a.m. appointment."

"Odd time for a meeting. And why meet at home rather than at his office? Well, enough shop talk. Looks like we're starting to trim the tree."

Evan and Mike, both holding red paper plates full of cookies, sat on the sofa and motioned for Susan to join them.

Satin put on holiday music and instructed the guests

to go to work. "No master plan. Just hang them wherever you think they'll look good."

Gabby and Daniel joined in the decorating. Susan was happy to see them both smiling. She picked up an ornament and threaded a metal hook through it. The gold circle featured a school she knew well.

"Westbrook Centennial. Satin, I didn't know you grew up around here. Are your parents still in town?"

"No, I'm afraid they've both passed on."

"I'm sorry."

"It's not a fresh wound. Hey, I think that ornament would look nice at the top, just under the angel."

Susan hung ornaments until her fingers felt numb. Threading the holders through the ornaments was a challenge, even with her bifocals, and her fingers weren't as nimble as they once were. After several glasses of nonalcoholic sangria, she excused herself to find the rest room.

"Knock, knock, anyone in there?"

"Yes, but there's another one at the end of the hall."

She followed the hallway, and erroneously made her way into a bedroom. After flicking on the light, she realized it was a man's room. The single bed was covered with a *Yankees* quilt, and clothes were strewn all over the floor. A faded red hoodie hung on the doorknob. *Obviously not the bathroom, but if Satin and Trey are living together, why aren't they sharing a room?*

She rejoined the guests and casually asked Trey if he lived there too.

"Yep. Why pay two rents when we're together all the time anyway?"

"Where are the kids sleeping?"

"There's a guest bedroom all set up for them. They're going to move in permanently during Christmas break so they don't have to change schools in the middle of the quarter. Satin's going to bring them to Westbrook Charter after the break."

"And are there wedding bells in the future?"

Mike and Evan found her before Trey, his face as red as his hair, could answer.

"Come on, Susan. Give the guy a break and stop being nosy." Mike handed her her jacket. "Looks like the party's breaking up. Ready to go?"

They said their good-byes and arrived home to a surprise on the front stoop.

Chapter 22

"Audrey? What are you doing out here in the cold? And how did you get here? I don't see your rental car."

Mike unlocked the door. "Let's get inside first. It's freezing out. Audrey, you're shaking."

"What's wrong, Grandma? I'll make you a cup of hot chocolate. Do you feel okay?"

"I had a fight with Richard, and I had to get away. I didn't know where else to go. I'd have called, but Richard smashed my phone. Good thing there was a taxi waiting outside the hotel."

Susan wasn't sure she'd heard correctly. "Smashed your phone? Why?"

"He was in the shower, and his phone vibrated. I looked at it and played the voice mail. It was a man named Bruce asking about 'the deal.' I confronted him when he got out of the shower, and he was furious. Said since I was sharing his phone, I didn't need mine, and he threw it against the wall, then smashed it with his boot. I was scared he was going to come after me next, so I ran out."

"Do you know who this guy is who called?" said Mike.

"He had a buddy in prison named Bruce. That's all I can think of."

"Bruce from prison. I'll call Lynette right now. She can send someone to pick up Richard and find out if Bruce is still in prison."

"Please don't. I need to go to bed. I'm exhausted. We can call her in the morning."

Susan reluctantly agreed, although falling asleep was no easy chore. She wished she could learn to let go of her worries at bedtime, but it never happened. What if Richard comes after Audrey and really hurts her? She wished they'd left him rotting in prison rather than proving him innocent.

In the morning, she struggled out of bed, hoping to catch a nap after lunch. Mike and Audrey were downstairs eating breakfast.

"Did you get any sleep, Audrey?"

"Not much. I'm thinking I overreacted. It really was none of my business, listening to that voice mail. I invaded Richard's privacy. I deserved his reaction."

Susan felt her face flush with anger. "Audrey, wake up! What's happened to you? Of course you don't deserve to be treated like garbage, especially by your own husband. When I first met you, you'd have never fallen into his trap. Even in Atlanta, when we were working on Richard's case, you were strong and confident."

"I'm just an old lady reaping what I've sown."

Mike brought a platter of pancakes to the table. "No self-pity allowed in this house, Audrey." He handed Audrey a plate. "I've been thinking. You have to be extra careful. Maybe you should stay with us. This Bruce character could prove dangerous. Especially if he's in prison and has connections."

"I'm going to call Lynette right now," said Susan. She gave Lynette the information and waited for a return call.

"I'm going to go back to the hotel. Mike, these pancakes are delicious, but I don't have much of an appetite."

Evan, still in his pajamas, came in and grabbed a plate. "What's going on? Did you talk to Richard?"

"I called Lynette and am waiting to hear what she

turns up regarding a prisoner named Bruce. Meanwhile, why don't we all go downtown and look at the holiday decorations? Barnes and Noble is having a big sale. We can browse and take our minds off things while we wait."

"I don't know. I'm not much in the mood for shopping."

"Come on, Grandma. I need dress clothes for the hospital, and you have great taste. Help me pick out a few things."

"Well... maybe for a little while."

By the time everyone was ready, the downtown stores were open. Main Street had been transformed into a Norman Rockwell Christmas scene, with wreaths hanging from the streetlights and a decorated Christmas tree in the middle of the town square. All it needed was a fresh sprinkling of snow.

They started with the bookstore. Susan's jaw dropped when she walked in and was greeted by a life-size cutout of Duncan Sitwell holding his new book, *Adios, America.* She picked up a copy of the book from the display table and read the back.

"How haven't I heard about this?" said Susan. "Duncan Sitwell, our very own town music teacher, has written a best-selling book! It's all about the negative influence of immigrants on American jobs. Can you believe it?"

Mike said, "You and I know that immigrants are mostly taking the jobs Americans don't want. And if they are illegal, they are extremely underpaid and often maltreated. Sensationalism always sells. People nowadays don't look below the headline."

"And the headline can be completely false. Back when I went to school, we were taught to check the source," said Audrey.

Susan flipped through the pages. "He mentions

Agrowmex. He says it's symbolic of what's wrong with our economy, and it should be demolished. Blames the CEO, who we all know was Matthew Chadwick, for bringing the company to the U.S."

Evan said, "Maybe he killed the Chadwicks to make a point and sell his book."

Mike picked up a copy from the table and turned to the title page. "Sure got it out fast. Did anyone at school know he was writing a book?"

"No," said Susan. "Not that I heard. And it sure made it to press quickly. Agrowmex has only been here a few months. It's his revenge for being bullied into selling his land to the company."

"Evan, why don't we go look at dress clothes?" said Audrey. "Mike and Susan, are you ready to go?"

"I'll catch up with you," said Susan. "I want to browse a bit."

Mike stayed behind with Susan and browsed through the sports books. Susan checked out the cozy mysteries, then wandered over to the psychology section. She pulled out a book called *Abuse is a Five-Letter Word.* The author, a clinical psychologist with a degree from Harvard, turned the word *abuse* into an acronym and divided the book into sections. Susan went to the *S* section on page fifty. *Spousal abuse*. She read the signs and mentally checked off every one on the list as they pertained to Audrey. The author said not to confront the abuser and to get the victim safely out of harm's way. *Easier said than done when the victim thinks she deserves the abuse.* She flipped to the resources section in the back of the book.

Mike came around the corner. "Are you ready to go?"

"Yes. Wait… shush. Do you hear that?"

"What?"

"That voice. It's Richard. He must have followed us.

Duck down." She listened to the conversation in the next aisle. Richard was talking.

"Yeah. From China to Mexico to here. Now it's your turn. This is the biggest shipment yet, and you'd better not mess it up. You don't want to mess with me or my partner, got it? Haven't I proven myself yet? I worked this down in Mexico, and it's running smoothly since I've been on this end of things. You're the newbie. Ask your partner. He'll tell you."

Susan grabbed Mike's arm and peeked around the stacks. She whispered, "That's Jordan Chadwick. Richard and Jordan are working together on something, and I'm willing to bet the partner's name is Bruce."

"Let's get out of here. Last thing you want is for Richard to see you."

They waited until they were sure the coast was clear, then caught up with Audrey and Evan at the clothing store. Susan looked in every direction, making sure Richard wasn't following her.

"Mom, look at these dress pants. They fit perfectly. My old black ones are too tight."

"Those are great. Are you ready to go?"

"I'll pay for these and then we're done," said Audrey.

Susan and Mike had decided not to tell Audrey they'd seen Richard in the bookstore. Susan was planning on having a heart-to-heart with her birth mother and convincing her to call the abuse hotline. On the way home, her phone vibrated.

"Lynette, do you have any news? Really? Recently released. He was Richard's cellmate? Consider him armed and dangerous? Okay, maybe I'm exaggerating, but I'll tell Audrey."

"What did she say?" asked Audrey.

"You heard the gist of it. Bruce Feinstein was Richard's cellmate the past ten years. He was in there for armed robbery and killed a store clerk in the process. He was recently released and lives here in Westbrook. Not the sort of friend you want your hubby hanging out with."

Audrey said, "Richard wouldn't put me in harm's way. Besides, we're going back to Florida soon."

Not believing what she was hearing, Susan said, "You can't be thinking of staying with him. Richard's an abusive jerk. My hairdresser's husband is a divorce lawyer. I'll put you in touch."

"Mom's right," said Evan. "I did a workshop at school on how to spot abuse."

"You're being overprotective, and I love you both for it, but by now Richard has calmed down and things will be back to normal."

When Mike pulled into the driveway, Richard's rental car was already parked on the swale. He was waiting for them on the stoop, holding a bunch of flowers.

"Audrey, I missed you. Let's go back to the hotel. I'll take you out for a nice romantic dinner."

To Susan's horror, Audrey ran into his arms, took the flowers, and gave him a smooch.

Mike said, "Let's all go inside."

"No, I want to take my bride home with me. Come on, Audrey."

Audrey got into the passenger seat next to Richard and waved as they pulled away.

Chapter 23

Going back to school after a five-day holiday was like jumping from a bathtub into the Atlantic in January. Even though she was a volunteer and could have easily opted to stay home, Susan knew Theresa depended on her. While she got dressed, she turned on the bedroom TV and saw a polished version of Duncan Sitwell being interviewed on the local news. His normal jeans and sweatshirt were replaced with a dark suit and fresh white shirt. He'd had a haircut, and his usual stubbly face was clean-shaven. The reporter announced he was slated to sign books at Barnes and Noble on Tuesday night. *Keep it up, Duncan. Spout your anti-immigrant, racist views for the whole town to hear.*

"Hey, Mike. What are we doing tomorrow night?"

"Nothing special. Why?"

"Want to go to Duncan Sitwell's book signing? Sooner or later he'll trip up and implicate himself in Matthew and Melissa's murders."

"So now he's your prime suspect? I thought Jordan was number one after what we heard at the bookstore."

"It's one of them or the other. I'm almost positive. After seeing Larry Frisina with his son at the tree lot, I don't think either of them is strong and clearheaded enough to have carried out two murders. Besides, Larry Frisina has an alibi for the night Melissa was killed. Think about it. I'll see you at dinner."

Susan almost ran a red light on the way to school. Even if Duncan Sitwell had been strongly urged into selling his land to Agrowmex, he had no right to offend the families who'd moved to a new country to continue working for the company. Did he think those employees leapt with joy at having to leave their homes and friends to keep their jobs?

What's wrong with people these days? What ever happened to the concept of loving thy neighbor? Neighbor? What about loving your own family? Every time she thought about Richard and how he was hurting Audrey, she wanted to throw something. *And then Audrey forgives him in a heartbeat.* She couldn't decide which made her blood boil more. When she parked at the school, she took a few deep breaths to calm herself before going inside.

Parents were lined up outside the principal's office. Susan heard them complaining about the "racist music teacher" while they waited to talk to Dr. Russo. In the mailroom, the buzz about Duncan Sitwell and his new book had everyone offering a take on the situation.

"I wonder if he's going to bother teaching music lessons anymore now that he's a famous author," said Stephanie. "I checked the voice mail this morning, and half a dozen parents left messages over the weekend asking what's going on. And they were lined up outside when I unlocked the school this morning. Most of the parents at our school are employed by Agrowmex and are deeply offended by his new book."

A young teacher carrying an armful of the controversial books said, "I'm very offended. My husband works for Agrowmex, and he's Mexican. I think the school should fire Duncan Sitwell. He shouldn't even be allowed on school property."

Stephanie said, "He wasted no time getting his book out. I'll bet he started writing the day we knew Agrowmex was coming to town."

"Can the school take out a restraining order on him?" asked Satin. "If it wasn't for Agrowmex opening in Westbrook, this school wouldn't even exist."

"I'll run it by my daughter," said Susan. She followed Satin upstairs to Theresa's classroom. "By the way, we had a lot of fun at your tree-trimming party the other night. And the twins are adorable. I think it's wonderful that you and Trey are taking them in just in time for the holidays."

"I'm excited about having them. Who knows, I may wind up adopting them if all goes well."

Theresa was writing instructions on the dry-erase board. "Who's adopting?"

"I'm getting ahead of myself," said Satin. "Susan was asking about Gabby and Daniel."

"You'd get to skip the sleepless nights and potty training if you do. They're at a nice age." Theresa grabbed a stack of artwork from her desk. "I almost forgot. Your sub left these with me to dry on Wednesday."

"Thanks," replied Satin. "Are we still making the hallway mural today? These are the decorations to put on our holiday scene. Wanted to make sure they had plenty of drying time."

"Yes," said Theresa, "after reading groups. Bring over your spray paints, and I've got garland, Christmas lights, a menorah, and an inflatable dreidel to hang from the ceiling."

Susan chatted with the students about their Thanksgivings while she monitored the reading centers. She already missed Evan, who'd flown back to St. Louis last night. She had no idea how long Audrey and Richard were staying. Now that Richard was connecting with Jordan Chadwick, she figured he'd be hanging around a while. Would he be able to convince Audrey to leave Banyan Beach? Susan would have said never had it been six months ago, but now... Richard had her under his spell.

"Mrs. Wiles, let's grab the decorations and the butcher paper. Time to deck the halls," said Theresa.

The students needed the pick-me-up after being home for four days. Susan and Satin held the butcher paper against the hallway while Theresa cut it and stapled it to the wall. Both teachers divided their kids along the length of the hallway, and the students grabbed art supplies and went to work.

"How is this going so smoothly?" asked Susan.

"We sketched it all out on Wednesday," said Theresa. "They know what parts they're responsible for."

A student came up to Theresa. "Can we have the red spray paint?"

Theresa rummaged through the cans Satin had taken out. "I don't see red. Hey, Satin, where's the can of red paint?"

"Isn't it there?" She rummaged through the box. "I guess I lost it when I made the move from my old school. Let's leave that section, and I'll pick up more on my way home."

Susan said, "I'm stopping at Walmart on my way home. I'll get some."

Lunchtime came and went. The students did a bit of math, then spent the afternoon finishing the mural—except for the parts that needed red paint.

"You know," said Satin, "if everything works out, Gabby and Daniel will be here painting next year's mural."

"It's the start of a Westbrook Charter tradition," said Theresa. "Isn't it fun being in on the ground floor. One day Ian may be coming here."

"If the school survives Duncan Sitwell's efforts to close down Agrowmex," said Susan.

"It'll blow over," said Theresa. "Hand me the step stool. If I stretch, I think I can hang the dreidel from the fluorescent lights. There. How does it look?"

"Beautiful," said Susan. "You put me in the Christmas spirit."

On her way out of the building, Susan saw Larry Frisina run past and jump into his truck. She poked her head back in the office.

"What's going on with Mr. Frisina? He was sure in a hurry, almost knocked me over as he was flying out the door."

"The hospital called and said it was an emergency. I got Mr. Frisina to the phone, and I heard him say, 'Chance, oh my God.' Then he ran out."

Chapter 24

As promised, on her way home, Susan stopped to pick up a can of red spray paint at Walmart, saving Satin the trip. The store had been decorated with garland, wreaths, and artificial trees the moment Halloween candy had gone half price, and now Christmas music streamed through the speakers.

She wondered how Chance Frisina was doing. How many brushes with death could one boy survive? Hopefully, he'd be home with his father by Christmas.

At the end of an aisle, Susan noticed a display of fitness watches on sale. She'd been semi-dedicated to her healthier lifestyle and on non-holiday days, managed to stay within her Weight Watchers points— mostly. *Maybe one of these will help me stay on track after all.* She browsed through the models and threw the one with the least bells and whistles into her basket.

"Susan Wiles. Theresa's helper, right?" Trey Carter was pushing a basket full of toys and child-sized sweatshirts.

"Trey Carter. Looks like you're in the Christmas spirit."

"Got out of work a little early and thought I'd take advantage of the time to do some Christmas shopping. It's a slow time of year for pest control."

"Pest control? Do you go around in the truck with the termite ears?"

Trey laughed. "No, I work for Bug Banishers, but I don't do the actual fieldwork. I'm a chemist. I spend my days developing safer, cheaper, and more effective ways to murder bugs and rodents."

"You and Satin make such a cute couple. Is there a ring in that basket, because this isn't the place to buy diamonds. I know a jeweler if you're in the market."

Trey blushed. "No ring in here, and thanks, but no thanks. I'd better get going."

"See you soon. Tell Satin I picked up the paint for tomorrow." She wheeled her way to the checkout line. On her way home, she called Lynette.

"Mom, what's up?"

"I'm stuck in traffic, so I thought I'd check in with you. Any news about Richard's friend?"

"Bruce Feinstein was released from prison last month. I talked to his probation officer, who verified Bruce is unemployed and living with his brother and sister-in-law."

"With no legal means of support. Did you find any connection to drugs? Any ties to Jordan Chadwick or Richard?"

"He had an arrest for selling drugs way back, and we know he and Richard were cellmates, so if I had to make a guess, I'd say there's a connection. Especially now with what happened to Chance Frisina."

"What happened? As I was leaving school, Larry rushed out in a big hurry."

"Another overdose. This time, Fentanyl. It's becoming an epidemic. Remember just last week the DEA stopped a truck heading into Vermont. They recovered enough Fentanyl to kill a small town."

"I'd never heard of that drug before."

"It's one hundred times more potent than morphine. It's often mixed with heroin because it's stronger and cheaper. The Mexican drug cartel has its hands in it. They get the raw materials from China, manufacture it in Mexico, then smuggle it into the U.S. for distribution."

"Agrowmex ships its products all over the Northeast. I saw trucks parked outside the plant when I was there. Lynette, you have to check it out. I bet the company is involved, especially with the Mexican connection."

"I'm a homicide detective, Mom. I'm sure the DEA has it under control. Don't you think they've considered the coincidence?"

"I guess so. But if it ties in with Melissa and Matthew's murders, it's your department."

"I hate when you act like I don't know how to do my job. Go home and cook a healthy dinner. I'll talk to you tomorrow."

When Susan got home, she told Mike about Chance's overdose and relayed the information Lynette had told her about Fentanyl. "Don't you think Agrowmex is involved? It's a no-brainer. And I'm sure it's tied into the two murders."

"There are big links missing in that chain. The police will work it out. What's in the bag?"

Susan pulled out her Fitbit. "It was on sale, so I thought I'd give it a try. Can you help me set it up?"

Mike got the watch started and explained to Susan, who lacked the patience for reading instructions, how to work it. "Let me see your phone. You can download an app and keep track of your progress. This is neat. It tells you the route you took, mileage, heart rate. I want one of these for Christmas."

"They're on sale. I'll let you know how I like it." She fastened it on her wrist. "What's that sound? What's it doing?"

"It's just your phone. Answer it."

"Audrey? What's wrong? Is he still there? Lock the door. We'll be right over."

Mike grabbed their coats. "I'm assuming Richard was at it again."

"He hit her and took off. Let's get to her before he

gets back."

They raced to the hotel and banged on the door. Tears streaming down her mascara-stained cheeks, Audrey fell into Susan's arms. "Thanks for coming so fast."

Mike said, "Come on. We're taking you to the emergency room. Then I'm going to call Lynette and have the police pick up Richard."

"No. I'm okay. I just need to wash my face."

"You're not okay. It's not normal to have your husband hit you. Ever. Mike is right. Let's go."

"Even if you're fine, we want the attack on record. The emergency room will document your injuries, and you'll have something to use against him when you file charges."

"File charges? I can't do that. He's my husband. Besides, it was my fault. I should have given in and agreed to sell my place in Florida."

"Listen to yourself! No one deserves to be abused. And if you want to stay in Florida, you should stay in Florida—with or without him."

Susan's voice was raw after trying her best to talk sense into Audrey. Mike handed Audrey her coat, and simply said, "Let's go." He led her out of the hotel room by the elbow. They were in the parking lot just as Richard returned.

"What are you doing with my wife? Where do you think you're taking her?"

Susan screamed, "We're taking her to the hospital you son of a... I wish we'd never gotten you out of prison. Did you beat your murdered wife too? If she hadn't been killed by someone else, I'll bet it was just a matter of time. A leopard doesn't change its spots."

Audrey broke free of Mike's grasp. "It's okay. I'm going inside with Richard now."

Red-faced and hoarse, Susan continued screaming,

"Oh no you're not. We're taking you to the hospital, and we're calling the police." She turned to Richard. "Maybe some of your old friends are still in prison and will be happy to be reunited with you. Too bad your buddy Bruce is on the outside, for now."

Richard swung at Susan. Mike jumped in between them and punched Richard in the eye.

Audrey screamed, "Stop! Everyone, just stop!"

The valet parking worker heard the commotion and ran over. "Do I need to call the police? Are you okay, sir?"

Richard brushed himself off. "I'm taking my wife back inside. If these two don't get in their car and leave this second, you can call the police."

"Are you kidding?" said Susan.

Mike grabbed Susan's hand. "Come on. We'll go home and call Lynette."

Stomping her foot, Susan looked at Audrey, hoping she'd come with them.

"Go on, Susan. I'll be fine." Audrey followed Richard back into the hotel.

Once in the car, Susan called Lynette but was informed they couldn't do anything to Richard unless Audrey filed charges. Lynette promised she'd have a talk with Audrey, but Susan wasn't satisfied. In her heart, she knew this wasn't going to end well.

Chapter 25

The next morning, Susan called Theresa and told her she wouldn't be coming in. She wanted to check on Audrey and vowed she would do whatever it took to convince her mother to press charges. Mike grabbed his lunch box and gave her a kiss.

"I know you're worried, but we've done all we can do. Audrey has to *want* to leave Richard, and she's not at that point."

"When will she be at that point? When he kills her? I'm going to call George down in Florida. Maybe he can talk some sense into her."

After Mike left, Susan called her half-brother, who filled her with more exasperating stories about their mother. "It's a pattern. He yells at her, storms out, then comes home with roses and she forgives him. I can't get her to see things clearly. Susan, believe me, I've tried. Now you say he hit her? Can you convince her to fly home without him? She can stay with me in case he follows her back."

"I'll try. Meanwhile, see if you can find a good therapist who deals with abuse cases. And a divorce attorney while you're at it."

"I'm on it. And you be careful. If Richard gets wind of your plan to get Audrey away from him, he'll be furious and he'll come after you."

Remembering that George was with the DEA, she said, "George, have you heard of a drug called Fentanyl?"

"Heard of it? Don't get me started. It's our biggest

enemy right now. It's coming up from Mexico and down from Canada. It's everywhere. Dealers mix it with heroin and unsuspecting addicts overdose. An amount the size of two grains of salt can kill a full-grown male."

"Do you know if it's popular in my area?"

"Oh, yeah. Like I said, it's spreading like wildfire. Why do you ask?"

"I think Richard is dealing it with his old cellmate and the son of the murdered CEO of Agrowmex."

"I wouldn't be surprised. Maybe he'll get thrown in jail again and we won't have to worry about Mom."

After she hung up, she tried Audrey but got voice mail. Noticing the Fitbit on her dresser, she decided to go for a walk. *Maybe I'll develop a strategy while I'm freezing my tail off outside.*

Susan's elderly neighbor was walking her dog, and their paths crossed.

"Susan, how are you? Surviving that house full of company? I've seen more cars in and out of your driveway these past few weeks than I have the entire last year."

"My birth mother and her husband are visiting from Florida, and my father is visiting too. Actually, at the moment he's in Atlanta packing his house. He'll be moving here to Westbrook."

"You must be excited. I'm glad our town's tarnished reputation isn't keeping newcomers away. It's been one thing after another. First Agrowmex moves in and it causes protests. Then the Chadwicks are murdered, and now it's drugs."

"Drugs?"

"I was talking to my daughter, who works at the hospital. She says she's seeing a wave of overdose admissions. Used to be rare. Sure, occasionally, you'd hear about a kid smoking pot, but rarely anything heavier."

"What's the new drug of choice? Did she say?"

"I don't remember the name, but it's the one that killed that singer Prince." Her little white dog pulled on the leash. "I'd better keep moving. Trixie doesn't have a whole lot of tolerance for the cold anymore. She's getting old like the rest of us."

Old like the rest of us? She picked up the pace, watching her heart rate increase on her Fitbit.

When she returned home, she again tried Audrey and was able to convince her to meet for lunch. Richard was "out with an old friend," so Audrey didn't think he'd mind. *Since when does she need permission?*

"Susan, how about that Italian place, Vinny's?"

As much as she could live on Italian food three meals a day, she said, "There's a new sandwich shop downtown. They make the bread fresh, and the soups are delicious."

Susan changed her clothes, then picked up Audrey at the hotel. In the car, she asked Audrey, "Where did you say Richard went?"

"He's hanging out with some friend. I didn't ask who."

"Looks like quite a bruise you've got there. You can't think it's okay for him to hit you, Audrey. I'll help you get away from him. So will Lynette."

"It'll be okay. Richard's a good man. He has a bit of a temper sometimes, that's all."

Downtown parking was scarcer than usual now that it was officially holiday shopping season. Susan found a spot a few doors down from The Savory Sandwich, cute with its green-and-white canopy and, "Tis the season... for soup" written on the window with fake snow. They passed several shoppers loaded down with bags.

"I'm so glad the small businesses downtown are

thriving, in spite of Walmart and the mall."

"In Florida, I do all my shopping at the mall," said Audrey. She followed her daughter into the café, where they were seated near the window.

Susan ordered a turkey sandwich on whole-wheat bread, counting up the points in her head. Her Fitbit registered 5,000 steps after her morning walk, and she felt encouraged to stick to her plan, in spite of current stressors. During lunch, she steered the conversation to the situation with Richard, but Audrey evaded her grilling and instead chatted about Evan, her great grandbabies, and selling her house in Banyan Beach.

"Why do you want to sell? Your home is beautiful, it's warm in Florida, you still enjoy working at the school you've headed for more than half your life, and your son is there."

"But I'll be closer to you and the girls. We'll be one big happy family."

Susan could barely stomach the thought of Audrey and Richard living in Westbrook. She prayed Richard would get arrested again and die in prison. She hadn't realized how her mind had wandered until Audrey nudged her.

"Susan, did you hear me? Do little girls still play with Easy-Bake ovens? I was thinking of getting one for Annalise for Christmas."

"She'd love that. She already helps Lynette in the kitchen by stirring ingredients. Do they still make those?"

"Why don't we run by Walmart and see? Oh, and we went past a bookstore. Let's look there too. Annalise is almost reading on her own already. Such a genius."

Susan never could resist a trip to a bookstore. When they walked in, a small crowd was gathered. She craned her neck to see who they were listening to. Being taller, Audrey read the cover of the books displayed in front of the speaker.

"Look, Susan. It's that author who wrote the anti-Mexico book. I saw him on *Good Morning, Westbrook* the other day."

"Duncan Sitwell? Who falls for that garbage he writes? Unless you came over on the Mayflower or are a Native American, you're an immigrant."

A woman next to her gave Susan a stern, "Shush."

Duncan continued. "This country must protect itself. Agrowmex has to go. Its dead CEO and his dead wife—let their deaths serve as a warning. Protect American jobs. Make your voices known by whatever means necessary."

The crowd clapped and cheered, sounding denser and more numerous than they were. Duncan Sitwell sat down behind the table of books, and a line formed in front of him as he picked up his pen. The comments she heard turned Susan's stomach. She heard someone ask if it was okay to engage violence if necessary, and Duncan's response was, "Absolutely."

"He's a lefty, just like Richard," said Audrey. "I wonder if his handwriting is just as difficult to read."

Surprised that Audrey focused on Duncan's left-handedness rather than his horrid comment, she nodded her head. "Too bad his book isn't illegible."

A worker came over and tried to make order out of the line. "Quite a crowd we've got on a weekday afternoon."

Susan said, "There are some strong feelings here in town regarding the book's subject matter."

"Yeah, but I've noticed a slight uptick after school too. Nice to know there are some high schoolers out there who still like to read. Mostly they browse, but it brings in business. Most don't leave without at least buying a latte."

Susan remembered seeing Jordan here recently,

secretly meeting with Richard. *How clever would it be to carry out drug deals in the middle of a bookstore?*

"Susan, I should be getting back to the hotel," said Audrey.

"Sure, let's go." When they got to the hotel, Susan insisted on walking Audrey to her room. There was no telling what kind of mood Richard would be in, if he was even back from his meeting.

"I don't need a babysitter, Susan."

"I know. I need to use the bathroom anyway." She followed Audrey into her hotel room. "Looks like Richard is still out." She put her purse down on the bed, checking her phone first in case Mike had tried to call. Reassured that Audrey was alone, she chatted for a few minutes, then started back home.

She was halfway to her house when she decided to call Lynette and tell her about Duncan and Richard both being left-handed. Surely Lynette would be able to check her reports and see if the fireplace poker had been used by someone left-handed. Maybe she could also tell if Melissa was strangled by a southpaw.

Darn, I don't have my phone. I'll bet it fell out of my purse when I left it on Audrey's bed. She turned the car around and headed back to the hotel. The sky was gray and gloomy with the sun already low in the sky. She pulled into the parking lot and noticed Richard talking on his phone in his rental car. Then Richard pulled out of the lot. *Where's he going? Audrey thought he'd be home already.* He gave no sign that he noticed Susan. *Maybe he's going to the bookstore to work a deal.* She made a split-second decision to follow him.

Chapter 26

Snow flurries fell on the windshield as Susan tailed behind Richard. She was convinced he was heading for the bookstore. *Late afternoon—I'll bet he's working a deal.* She was ready to turn onto Main Street, but Richard surprised her, heading in the opposite direction. She kept two cars behind him, sure he wouldn't be able to tell it was her, especially with the snow falling more heavily. *He's heading toward Agrowmex.*

She slowed down as he approached the nearly deserted company, then pulled in behind a blue Toyota. She turned into the far end of the parking lot, parked behind a tree and watched.

A young man in a parka exited the car. *Jordan Chadwick. I knew it!* Richard got out of his car and met with Jordan right in the middle of the lot. First they talked. It killed her not to be able to hear the conversation. Then Richard grabbed a package from his car and handed it to Jordan. Jordan pointed toward the loading dock around the side of Agrowmex. Richard got back into his car and pulled out onto the main road. Jordan pulled around to the loading dock.

I have to see what he's up to. I'll call Lynette. Then she realized that her phone was still in Audrey's hotel room. She evaluated the risk of following him without backup, against the chance she'd miss catching him red-handed in a drug deal. She went with her gut and followed him, promising herself she'd keep her distance.

When she got near the dock, she turned off the

engine. Then the road shook as a large trailer truck pulled in. Jordan got out of his car and jogged over to it. He greeted the driver, then climbed up the loading platform and opened the back. Jordan waved the driver on.

The driver, hood pulled tight over his head, scarf around his face, walked across the loading area, chirped his keys, and got into his own car. Like Richard, he pulled away onto the main road. Jordan stood on the platform behind the truck. She watched him grab a dolly and start unloading boxes.

What's in those boxes? I have to get a closer look. She hugged the building and scooted around to where the truck was parked. Now it was snowing heavily, and at this time of year, it was already getting dark outside, helping to hide her from Jordan. She ducked down and went to the far side of the truck, inching her way closer to the back of the trailer. *I have to get a peek, then I'll go home and call Lynette.*

Jordan pushed a dolly full of boxes back into the truck. While he was inside, she gingerly crept up the metal platform steps to truck height and peeked her head around the back opening of the trailer. Her boot slipped, and she had to grab the side of the truck to keep herself upright. Her heart nearly stopped for a moment while Jordan froze and listened. *God, please don't let him find me.* She contemplated making a run for it, but her near tumble on the slippery steps gave her pause. She held her breath…

Finally, Jordan continued, then wheeled the empty dolly back onto the platform. Susan stepped back down and onto the pavement. *Phew. That was a close call.* She walked around the truck. As she was about to go across the cab and have a clear shot to the parking lot, she felt a sharp blow and collapsed to the ground like a deflating bounce house. That's the last thing she remembered before waking up in ice-cold darkness.

Where am I? My head is killing me. Not an ounce of light permeated her surroundings. She felt the coldness of a floor and crawled until she felt a wall. That's when realization hit. *I'm in the back of the truck! Help, help!*

The complete darkness made her panic. She shivered both from cold and fright as she crawled around to find the door. She pulled the handle, but it was locked from the outside. Her breathing was rapid, and she worried she was about to have a panic attack. Then she remembered the Fitbit on her wrist and hit the button. *Thank God.* A small bit of light was immensely better than none at all.

She banged on the door, screaming, though she knew no one would hear her. *By now they'll be looking for me.* She imagined Mike wondering where she was, then calling Lynette, who would probably call Audrey... then what? *Audrey will say I went home. No one will think to look for me at Agrowmex, and with the storm outside, workers may not even show up tomorrow.*

When her fists were too bruised to bang and her voice too hoarse to scream, she grabbed her knees and huddled by the door. Eventually someone would find her. *I'm sure I can last a day or two without food and water.* She had a brainstorm. *This is a produce plant. Maybe there's actual produce in all these boxes.*

She pulled herself to her feet, head still throbbing from the blow. She felt along the wall and came to a stack of crates. She reached her gloved fingers inside one, but there was no way to open it. She thought she felt glass and guessed it was a crate of apple juice or cider. Resolved to wait for help—hungry, cold, and with a monster headache, she sat back down on the floor, fighting tears.

She was so fatigued she drifted in and out of sleep, dreaming of her granddaughters and her nice, warm house. She imagined Ludwig and Johann nuzzling next to her. And of course Mike. *He must be worried sick by now.*

After what seemed like hours, she heard a banging on the outside of the door. *Help! I'm in here!* She had a terrifying thought. *What if Jordan is coming back to finish me off?*

"Mom, are you okay?" Lynette ripped open the doors of the truck, carrying a flashlight. Mike and Jackson were with her. "What on earth are you doing here?"

"I was going to call you but…"

"But you left your phone in Audrey's hotel room. Mom, when will you learn? I thought you were getting better about taking risks, and now here you are, up to your old tricks."

"I didn't want to lose him. I followed Richard, and he met with Jordan Chadwick, right here in the parking lot. They're dealing drugs and using Agrowmex as a cover. Check the crates. I'll bet you'll find evidence."

"You know you had me scared to death, and again it didn't matter to you," said Mike.

She hugged him. "I'm so sorry. I didn't mean to. How did you find me anyway?"

Mike stiffened, not ready to forgive and forget just yet. "Your Fitbit. We went to Audrey's and found your phone under the bedspread. When I checked it, I hit the Fitbit button, and it showed your route. We found you from there."

"Then Fitbit actually saved my life. I should do a commercial for them."

"Not funny. I'm still angry."

Jackson went to the car and returned with a crow bar. He pulled apart crates, while Lynette led Susan out of the truck and into the warm police car, where they called Audrey to tell her Susan was safe. Susan told Lynette about Duncan Sitwell at the bookstore and how the woman who worked at the store said high school kids hung out there after school.

"And Duncan Sitwell spews venom about Agrowmex. He even said Matthew and Melissa deserved to die—if not in those exact words. And another thing. He's left-handed. So is Richard. I'll bet the blow that killed Matthew and the strangulation of Melissa was by someone left-handed. I'm right, aren't I?"

"No, Mom. The killer in both cases was right-handed. Do you think I didn't check the autopsy reports? And you don't make sense. First you say Jordan is the killer because of drugs, and in the same sentence, you tell me you think it was Duncan Sitwell because he's left-handed and hates Agrowmex for taking American jobs."

"I'm sorry. The blow to my head may be worse than I thought." The car door opened.

"Lynette, bingo," said Jackson. "There are baggies full of fine, white powder under the bottles of apple cider."

"I'll call the station and have them pick up Jordan Chadwick, both for drugs and for assaulting my mother."

"What about Richard?"

"We don't have solid evidence linking him to the drugs. All you saw was him handing over a package to Jordan Chadwick. We need more than that."

Jackson said, "All's not lost. I'm betting Jordan implicates Richard when we interrogate him. Especially if he thinks he'll get off easier."

Susan leaned her head on Mike's shoulder. "Can we go home now? I'm starving, and I have fifteen points worth of food left. Let's call for pizza delivery on the way."

Chapter 27

School was canceled the next day due to the snowstorm. Susan stayed curled under her quilt, thinking about the events of the previous night. She wondered what Jordan had revealed in the police interview. Had he admitted to killing his parents as well as dealing drugs? Did he implicate Richard?

She went downstairs, fed the cats, and poured herself a cup of coffee. Mike had left the coffeemaker on for her. She knew he was still angry at her for following Richard and putting her safety at risk, but the fact that he made enough coffee for both of them meant he was softening. She didn't mean to be so impulsive and worry her loved ones. In fact, she thought she was making great progress—until yesterday.

Stop and think it through next time. Even if Richard got away, the police would eventually catch up to him and find out if he and Jordan were working together. Right? She lingered over a bowl of oatmeal, then called Lynette.

"What happened last night? Did Jordan confess to killing his parents?"

"Mom, he didn't kill his parents. His drug dealing gave him an alibi. An Agrowmex truck driver confirmed that Jordan was at the factory when he pulled in with his truck the night Melissa was killed."

"What about when Matthew was killed?"

"He was in class at the university. His professor confirmed it."

"So Jordan didn't kill his parents because he has an

alibi for both murders. Duncan Sitwell is left-handed, and the murder weapon was used in both cases by someone right-handed, so he's in the clear. What about Larry Frisina?"

"He's had his hands full with that son of his. When Matthew was murdered, he was driving Chance to a rehab in New Jersey, near where his ex-wife lives. As a matter of fact, he told me he plans to move to New Jersey at the end of the school year if not sooner. He and his ex-wife agreed that Chance will need the support of both his parents and a new environment to stay drug-free."

"Della Hops?"

"Mom, seriously?"

"Then where are you as far as suspects go? Agrowmex was being used by amateur butchers to start an illegal side business, it was used to transport drugs, and it supposedly took American jobs. None of those are motives? Then why were the CEO of the company and his wife murdered?"

"We don't know yet. We have to go in another direction. Be patient, Mom."

"Okay. I'll try. Meanwhile, did you pick up Richard for his involvement with the drugs?"

"No. Jordan refused to name anyone else. Says he was working alone. If he was involved, he'll eventually slip up. They always do."

Feeling unsatisfied, Susan unloaded the dishwasher, then ran the vacuum. What other motive was there? Maybe it had nothing to do with the company? Was that possible?

Just as she turned off the vacuum, her phone rang.

"Audrey, is everything okay?"

"Everything is wonderful. I've decided to sell my place in Florida and will be living in Westbrook early in the new year."

"I thought we talked about this. You have a beautiful place in Florida without snow and ice to worry about. You can swim practically all year long, and your son lives there. Have you told him what you're planning?"

"I wanted you to be the first to know."

"Why the rush?"

"Richard says he has a business opportunity here with his old friend, and he needs to be situated here quickly."

If she only knew it was a drug-dealing business. "I think you should call George and tell him your plans. You love Florida. Don't make a move you'll regret."

"I love Richard more. If he's happy, I'm happy. Gotta go. When Richard gets home, we have an appointment with a realtor. I'll let you know when we find something."

Let me know how it goes? The realtor certainly won't dissuade her. She called George.

"George, Audrey is about to do something terrible. She's putting her house on the market and is moving here! She says Richard has a business opportunity. I saw him making a deal with someone who was arrested just last night. Richard's lucky he was out of there in time."

"I'll check with my contacts in Florida and see if Richard's on their radar. Susan, you and I both know she's making a huge mistake—just like when she married the guy. She didn't listen to us then either."

"You've got to try."

"I'll see what I can do. Thanks for letting me know."

Susan flopped down on the sofa. She had nothing left in her bag of tricks to get Audrey to stay in Florida. She fell asleep watching her soap opera, waking up hours later when Mike came home.

"Have a restful afternoon?"

"Yes. How are the roads?"

"They're already clear. Even this morning, it wasn't too bad. Did you talk to Lynette?"

"Jordan is under arrest, but the police can't tie Richard into the drug business. At least not yet. Get this. Audrey has definitely decided to move to Westbrook. Richard says he has a business opportunity. Can't Audrey see what he's up to?"

"Love is blind. For example, I look right past your smile lines and love handles."

She gave him a swat. "That's because I have so many good things going for me. What does she see in Richard? He's abusive, he's a drug dealer, and now he's talking her into leaving the home she spent years making her own."

"Wish I had an answer. Are you ready for dinner?"

"Where are you taking me? I meant we should start cooking, but I'm easily swayed. Vinny's?"

"Sounds good. I've been cooped up in the house all day."

She changed into black stretch pants and an oversized sweater. In the car, she told Mike about her conversation with George and how he was going to ask his colleagues if they knew anything about Richard's involvement with drugs. The Christmas lights and the new fallen snow made the street look like a winter wonderland. She loved the festiveness of the holiday season.

Vinny's was crowded for a weeknight. After a short wait, they were seated near the window, with a view of Main Street that looked like the backdrop of a Hallmark Channel movie. Susan ordered angel hair pasta and a salad, with light balsamic dressing on the side. Mike opted for the linguine with sausage. Since his heart attack, he rarely ate high-fat meats, but every few months he treated himself.

Satin and Trey were seated across the room from

them. Susan waved, but they didn't see her from where they were seated.

"I've been thinking…" Susan drummed her fingers on the table.

"About Audrey or about the murders?" said Mike.

"The murders. I'm trying to connect the dots, knowing we've ruled out all the likely suspects. Who was dressed in the clown costume and left me that threat on Halloween? Who spray-painted the message on Matthew's house? Melissa had hired a private investigator, and the information she got showed that Chance and Jordan were involved in a drug deal. Matthew, Larry, Chance, and Jordan have all been cleared of both murders."

"The spray-painted message had nothing to do with the drug deals. The motive seems to have been Agrowmex's farming practices, particularly the amateur meat business."

"Those thugs were caught, and Matthew was cleared of involvement. Why kill him?"

"The immigrant issue. That's a motive."

"But…"

"I know. Duncan Sitwell had an alibi, and Lynette thinks it was beyond the capabilities of Della Hops and the hippies."

"Matthew planned to meet someone the morning he was killed. I saw what looked like an eight on his calendar for that day. I think it meant he had an eight a.m. appointment with someone he wasn't afraid of, right?"

"Not necessarily. Suppose a reporter called to interview him, or he was conducting an interview and wanted to keep it from the people at the company. Maybe he was trying to replace someone there."

Susan excused herself to use the restroom before the food came. On her way back to the table, she walked by

Satin and Trey, who were busy perusing the menus.

Satin said, "Susan—enjoying a night out with your hubby? I had nothing in the house to make, and I know the shelves at ShopRite have been picked clean with people preparing for last night's storm."

"It doesn't take much to convince me to opt for Vinny's over cooking. You look nice, all dressed up for your date with this handsome guy."

Trey blushed the color of his top. Susan couldn't remember seeing a man actually blush before, but Trey's light, freckled skin couldn't hide it.

"She always looks good. Me, however, I threw on this sweatshirt and the jeans that were draped over the chair from last night."

"She'll be a beautiful bride someday. You know, wedding season is just around the corner."

Clearing her throat, Satin said, "Do you think the police are any closer to finding out who killed the Chadwicks? I heard Larry Frisina and his son have moved to New Jersey. Guess he's off the suspect list."

"I heard he took his son to rehab and is planning on moving, but he might finish out the year in Westbrook. I don't know what his contract says. Jordan Chadwick is in the clear too. In the clear for murder, but sitting in a jail cell nonetheless for dealing Fentanyl. On a different note, what a pretty necklace you're wearing. Was it a gift from Trey?"

"No, I bought this myself at a craft fair. It had a matching bracelet, but I lost it somewhere."

Susan noticed the food arriving to her table. "I'll see you at school, Satin. Good seeing you again, Trey."

She sat back down across from Mike and dug into her food. "I'm starving." She gobbled down her pasta in a flash, then briefly contemplated dessert. *Nope. I'll wait until the weekend to have a treat. My pants already feel looser.* The waitress came by, and the suggestion of coffee was a decent compromise. She figured with enough cream, she could almost feel like she was having dessert.

Chapter 28

At school the next morning, the kids were wild from having had the previous day free. Snowstorms, rain, a full moon—the slightest change could tip the balance between sane and cabin-fever crazy. She passed overheated students bundled in jackets and scarves, lined up in the hallways, waiting for the bell to ring. She continued upstairs and found Theresa sitting at her desk, flipping through the elementary school yearbook.

"I never heard of putting out a yearbook in December!"

"Dr. Russo says it's more of a 'welcome to our new school' book. Something to introduce parents to the faculty and students."

Susan looked over Theresa's shoulder and pointed to a photo. "Is that you?"

"I know. I haven't changed a bit since fourth grade." She laughed. "We had to submit pictures of us at the age we're currently teaching."

Satin came in. "Is that the yearbook? Can I see?" She turned the page. "Oh God, I look so dorky. I was lucky to find a picture from back then."

Susan said, "You were adorable in those pink flowered overalls!"

The kids started coming into the room. "See you at lunch," said Satin.

While she circulated and helped the students, something tugged at Susan's mind. She couldn't put her finger on it, so she occupied herself with answering questions and setting up new reading centers.

After school, she stopped at Lynette's house to see Annalise and Mia. Lynette had the day off—a rarity since the murder investigations had started. She knocked on the door, and Annalise grabbed her around the thighs.

"Grandma, look what I'm making!" The tot led Susan to the kitchen table, where she was assembling beaded necklaces from a kit she'd received as a birthday gift. "Don't spill the beads onto the floor, Grandma. Mia will choke on them."

Lynette walked into the kitchen, holding Mia. "That's right. Mia is a turbo crawling machine these days, and everything she finds in her path goes straight into her mouth."

Susan examined the work in progress. "That's beautiful, honey. It's going to match those pink overalls I bought you." She turned to Lynette. "Any new leads in the case?"

"We're brainstorming alternative motives. We did get the lab report back from the parts of the bomb that exploded at Melissa's memorial service. It was a homemade concoction made from pesticides and sulfur. Like I said before, it was meant to create havoc, but if the perpetrator had wanted to cause massive destruction, he'd have used something more potent."

Susan's phone rang. "Yes, Audrey. I'm at Lynette's right now. You're kidding. You haven't even put your Florida house on the market. I urge you to think some more about it. I'll give them kisses from you."

Lynette said, "Don't tell me. She and Richard bought a house here in Westbrook."

"They made a bid on one. I guess George couldn't talk sense into her either." Annalise brought over the necklace she was making. "Grandma, can you tie this?"

"Sure, honey." As she tied the beads, she had a flash image of the beaded necklace that Satin was wearing at

Vinny's. "Lynette, did you ever find out who owned the beads that were found on Matthew's stoop?"

"No. They're still sitting in evidence. We couldn't get prints off them. Why?"

"Nothing. Annalise's necklace reminded me of it." She had to see Satin's jewelry again to be sure. *Satin said she used to have a matching bracelet, but she lost it.*

"Mom, I have to get dinner started. Do you want to stay? You can call Dad and tell him to come."

"Thanks, but Dad won't be home until late tonight. The permits office got behind due to some employees not wanting to brave the roads yesterday. I have to go." She kissed her granddaughters good-bye.

Satin's place is on the way home. What excuse do I have for stopping by though? She drove in the direction of Satin's. On the way, she remembered she'd put a bag of old sweaters and blankets in the trunk to donate to Satin's foster-child clothing drive. It had been in the back for weeks already, and she kept forgetting to bring them in to school.

What possible connection did Satin have to the Chadwicks? Satin had left early the night of the open house, meaning she had the opportunity to kill Melissa. Satin was also late to work the day Matthew was killed. And what if it wasn't an eight *but an* S *I saw on his calendar? Did he have a meeting scheduled with Satin the day he was killed?*

She pulled up in front of Satin's and grabbed the bag of clothing from the back. Then she remembered why she was stuck on the idea of overalls. In the photo for the Westwood Charter yearbook, Satin had been wearing pink flowered overalls in the photograph. *The picture!* She put her phone in her pocket and rang the doorbell.

"Susan? What are you doing here? Please, come in."

"I've been lugging around this bag of clothing in my car for weeks, meaning to bring it to you at school. I have some sweaters and blankets for the clothing drive."

"You're a doll, but you didn't have to make a special trip. Can I get you some coffee?"

"Sure. Coffee sound good. Do you mind if I use your bathroom?"

"Of course not. Down the hall next to my bedroom."

Satin's bedroom door was wide open. From the hallway, Susan saw jewelry lying on her dresser. *I'm going to take a really quick peek.* The floor creaked. She froze, hoping Satin hadn't heard it. She heard the water running in the kitchen. *If she catches me in here, I'll just say I went into the wrong doorway.*

Susan tiptoed in and scanned the dresser. She saw a watch, several pairs of earrings, and just what she was looking for—the necklace that Satin had worn to dinner the other night. She adjusted her bifocals and bent over to look at it. *I'm almost sure this matches the beads I found on the ground when I went to see Matthew.*

She scurried out of the room and darted into the bathroom. She started to call Lynette but thought better of it. *Lynette will ask why I snuck into Satin's bedroom and will say I should leave it to the police. I have to put the pieces together before I talk to her.*

She made it back to the living room just as Satin brought in a mug of coffee from the kitchen. "Here you go. Nice and hot."

"Do you and Trey have plans for winter break?"

"I'm bringing Gabby and Daniel here to live. We'll be helping them adjust, maybe take them ice skating or to the bounce-house place. Do you think they're too old for that?"

"I've been there with Annalise. They have a separate side with trampolines for the older kids. I bet they'll love it."

"I don't know. I read an article about kids getting injured on trampolines."

"They can't live in a bubble, as much as it would be a great relief if they could. What about Christmas? Are you going to visit your family, or are they in town?"

"My parents are no longer alive."

"I'm sorry, I forgot. What about Trey's family?" asked Susan.

"No longer in the picture."

"Sorry to hear that. Where is Trey anyway?"

"He's still at work at Bug Banishers. He'll be home soon."

"That's right. He's a chemist. He told me he develops pest poisons. I'll bet he comes home with chemicals spilled all over his clothes for you to clean up. Stinky too, right?"

"He wears old clothes in the lab, unless he has a meeting. And yes, some of the chemicals he uses stink. Thank goodness for extra-strength laundry detergent."

"Like that red sweatshirt he had on at Vinny's? I noticed a spot on the sleeve."

"He practically lives in that sweatshirt. It's older than dirt. Do you want more coffee?"

"No, I'm good." Susan took a sip, then changed the subject. "The police say neither Agrowmex nor the illegal side businesses associated with it were the motive for Melissa and Matthew's murders. I was sure it had to be. After all, what other reason would someone have for killing the two of them?" She carefully watched Satin's expression.

"I don't know. Enemies from back in Mexico?"

"Did you know the two of them well? This is so strange, but I went to visit Matthew Chadwick about the memorial scholarship that he wanted to establish in his wife's honor, and outside his front door, I saw beads scattered, like someone's bracelet broke apart right outside the front door. Here's the strange part. They looked like they were a perfect match for the necklace you had on at Vinny's. Didn't you say you had a matching bracelet but lost it?"

"What are you implying, Susan? I barely knew Melissa from school, and I never even met Matthew Chadwick. Do you think I'm involved in the murders?"

"Of course not. I'm thinking someone who knew the Chadwicks well enough to visit you, may have found or even stolen your bracelet. The beads are very unique."

"I wrote off that bracelet long ago. Now I should start dinner before Trey comes home." She got up and handed Susan her coat. When she opened the front door, Trey was standing there.

"Hey, Susan. School business after hours?"

"No, I was just dropping off a bag for the clothing drive." Trey and Satin stood side by side. "I never noticed how much the two of you look alike."

Trey said, "You know what they say. Hang around someone long enough and you start looking alike."

Susan didn't buy it. *The overalls! Satin was wearing the same pink overalls in her yearbook picture as the girl in the photo that Melissa Chadwick had locked in the school safe. And they looked like the same, redheaded girl.*

"Good to see you again. Careful driving home." He held the door open.

Susan looked back and forth between Satin and Trey. "You know, the two of you could pass for brother and sister." It hit her like a burst of steam. *The boy in the picture is Trey! Why did Melissa Chadwick have a picture of them in her possession? She kept it locked away after all these years. It must have meant something to her.*

"Something wrong, Susan? You got a strange look

on your face."

"I'm fine. I'd better get home."

Trey slammed the door shut before she could leave. "Tell us why you're really here."

"I came to drop off…"

"I said, why you're really here."

Satin said, "She thinks we had something to do with the murders. She found beads on the Chadwick's doorstep and thinks they're mine. Now she seems to be implying we're lying about our relationship."

"Did you?" said Susan. "You don't have an alibi for either murder, and Trey works with chemicals. He could have made the bomb that exploded at Melissa's funeral service. And the spray paint! Satin, you had full cans of spray paint for your class to use except for the red. The red was empty, and the message spray-painted on Matthew's house that said *murderer* was painted in red."

"You should start a second career as a fiction writer," said Trey.

Susan continued. "If you and Satin are a couple, why do you have separate bedrooms?"

"Let's tell her. She's obviously not going to let this go. Satin and I are brother and sister. Our real mother was a heroin addict, and our father was a lifer in prison. After our mother's lethal overdose, our father relinquished his parental rights. At least that's what our new parents told us."

Susan held her coat over her arms. She wiggled the phone from her pocket, keeping it hidden.

Satin continued. "Melissa and Matthew Chadwick took us in as foster parents. Melissa couldn't get pregnant. We became a family. Christmas presents, beach vacations—just like a real family."

Trey said, "Then one night after dinner, they sat us down and said they had a surprise for us. They were going to officially adopt us. Melissa had baked a cake and written *Our Forever Family* on it."

"Melissa even bought one of those silly stickers for the car, with stick figures representing the four of us."

"So what happened? Did they adopt you?"

"Nope," said Trey. "Days before the adoption was to be finalized, Melissa found out she was pregnant. They said it was a miracle—a sign from God."

"They sent us back to foster care. They couldn't handle three children with their busy careers and all. Truth is, they wanted their perfect family, without raising someone else's trash."

"And look how perfect it was," said Trey. "Melissa gave birth to drug-dealing, good-for-nothing Jordan. Perfect family, my foot. I believe God punished them for giving us back by giving them Jordan as a son."

"And you were angry, so you murdered them?" said Susan.

"We were angry. No one wanted to adopt a nine-year-old and her ten-year-old brother. They all wanted babies or at least toddlers. We grew up being shifted from house to house, then finally landed in a group home."

"They threw us out the minute Trey turned eighteen. They were going to keep me for one more year, but I wasn't going to lose the only family I had, so I ran away. Trey and I lived on the streets."

"You both got college degrees. Someone was watching out for you."

"My biology teacher at school knew the whole story. He helped me register for the SAT and fill out college applications. Even found scholarships for both of us. He changed our lives."

"Then why go after the Chadwicks after all those years? You both have good jobs and a roof over your heads."

"We had made peace with it. We still carried the scars, but when we heard Melissa and Matthew were moving back to Westbrook, we decided to try to meet with them and tell them we forgave them."

Susan said, "You forgave them by killing them?"

"No," said Satin. "We ran into them at the grocery store. Practically bumped our cart right into them. They didn't even recognize us. Said 'excuse me,' and moved on."

"I understand. I'd better be getting home." Her legs were trembling as she moved toward the door.

"Not so fast," said Trey. He pushed her down onto the couch. "Looks like Westbrook will see another murder. After three, it becomes a serial killer terrorizing the town. Only, after we get rid of you, we're good. No more murders."

"Why did you have to kill them?" Her mind was split between listening to the story and figuring out an escape plan.

"We went to meet with Melissa the night of open house. She came into my classroom and then realized who I was. She said to come to their house right away and we'd talk. That's why I left early, and so did she."

Trey said, "She didn't want Matthew to know about us yet and was afraid he may have come home early from his business trip. She wanted to soften the impact, so we agreed to pick her up at her house and go somewhere quiet to talk. In the car, we started talking, and it was clear Melissa had no regrets about sending us back to foster care. Didn't say she was sorry or that she was glad to see we'd turned out okay."

Satin said, "Then she tried to write us a check, to disappear. She didn't want the story getting out. I was furious, and Trey just snapped. Good thing he wasn't driving, or we all would have wound up going over the side of the railroad bridge."

"I was sitting in the back seat. She was wearing a scarf. I pulled it tighter and tighter until she stopped moving. When we were convinced she was dead, we threw her over the railroad bridge and dumped her purse in the woods."

The sound of the cuckoo clock made them all jump. Susan saw her opportunity. She unplugged a lamp and bashed Trey with it. She ran to the front door, grabbed the handle, and ran outside, dropping her phone on the snow.

Trey followed her. "You're not going anywhere! Get back inside!" He shoved her hard back onto the couch. "Don't you want to hear the end of the story?"

Satin said, "I decided to give Matthew a chance. After all, I was a real daddy's girl back then. I set up an appointment to meet him at his house before school. I told him who I was, and you know what he did?"

"What did he do?" Her heart was thumping. *Keep stalling them until you figure out how to escape.*

"The same thing as Melissa! He offered me money to disappear. I grabbed the fireplace poker and swung it hard at his head. He fell, and when I saw the blood, I panicked. I dropped the poker, then remembered even in my panic, to wipe off my fingerprints. When I pulled the door behind me, my bracelet got caught and the beads flew everywhere. I never expected anyone to notice them."

"Now to get rid of you. What sounds better, dying from a blow to the head or strangulation?"

"Trey, hitting her head will make a mess like it did when I killed Matthew."

"Strangulation it is." He grabbed a scarf from the coat tree and wrapped it around Susan's neck. She struggled to get away, but he was too strong. She began praying.

The door flew open. Lynette and Jackson ran inside,

guns poised. "Drop it."

Lynette untangled the scarf. Susan coughed, then grabbed her daughter. "How did you know where to find me?"

"Your phone line was open. You must have tried calling and forgotten to hang up."

"I did. Thank God."

Lynette and Jackson cuffed and Mirandized Trey and Satin before leading them into the squad car. Lynette drove Susan home in the Prius. Mike ran to the door, too happy to see his wife safe to be angry.

Chapter 29

Christmas dinner was on the table. Evan came in from St. Louis a few days earlier and helped with the preparations. Lynette strapped Mia into the highchair while Jason helped Annalise crawl into the booster seat. Jonathan had closed on his new house the previous week, and Susan was thrilled he was enjoying the first of many holidays with them. He'd even brought a friend.

"Janet, we're so happy you came," said Susan. "And I love your snazzy new hairdo."

"I'm delighted Jonathan invited me." Janet patted his thigh as she spoke. "I haven't celebrated Christmas since my husband died. My son and his wife are military, stationed in the Philippines. What's a holiday without family around?"

"You're always welcome here," said Susan. "Jonathan tells me you were a great help setting up his new house."

"It was a delight. I'm glad he's moved into a once-again peaceful Westbrook. Agrowmex named a new CEO. I hear he's announced plans to open dozens of new jobs earmarked for Westbrook residents. That'll shut Duncan Sitwell up."

Lynette said, "Gabby and Daniel have been adopted by two of Jason's colleagues at the college."

Jason said, "Mary and Pat are both math professors and have wanted children for a long time. Those kids are in great hands. Pass the mashed potatoes, please."

"I want more stuffing, Grandma."

Susan scooped stuffing onto her plate. "Did Santa eat the cookies you left out for him?"

"Yep. And the milk too. I got a real oven from Great-grandma."

"Speaking of Audrey, when are they getting back from Florida?" said Evan.

"They were supposed to come in late last night. I told them to come by after they get themselves settled. I won't ever love seeing Richard at this table." Her phone vibrated. "Speak of the devil."

"Mom, during dinner?" chided Lynette.

"I just want to make sure they got back safely. Hi, Audrey. Are you back in Westbrook?"

"Susan, I'm… I'm—"

"Audrey, what's wrong? You're scaring me."

"I'm… I'm in jail."

"Jail? Did they arrest Richard? They finally caught him red-handed dealing drugs. You can still come over. He's not going anywhere."

"No, you don't understand. I'm the one in jail. I've been arrested for killing Richard."

Susan's arm dropped, almost losing the phone.

"Mom, what's wrong?" said Lynette. "You look like you've just seen a ghost."

Evan said, "Mom, are you okay?"

"It's Audrey. She's… she's been arrested. She says she killed Richard."

"Mom, that's crazy. She must mean she's finally had it with him." Lynette sighed.

Susan looked down at the phone, and remembering Audrey was still on the line, put it to her ear. "Slow down, Audrey. You don't mean you actually killed him?"

"Mom, dinner's getting cold. Hang up and call her back later," said Lynette.

"Yes, Audrey. We'll be right there." She ended the

call, placing the phone on the table.

Mike shook his head. "Not on Christmas…"

Janet said, "Does this mean you have a new case to solve?"

Jonathan's face changed from concerned to excited as he stood up and headed toward the door, followed by Susan and Janet.

Mike put down his fork. "Here we go again."

THE END

ABOUT THE AUTHOR

 Diane Weiner is a veteran public school teacher and mother of four children. She has enjoyed reading for as long as she can remember. She has fond memories of reading Nancy Drew and Mary Higgins Clark on snowy weekend afternoons in upstate New York and yearned to write books that would bring that kind of enjoyment to her readers. Being an animal lover, she is a vegetarian and shares her home with two adorable cats and a little white dog. In her free time, she enjoys running, attending community theater productions, and spending time with her family (especially going to the mall with her teenage daughter and getting Dairy Queen afterwards).

Murder Is Chartered is the eighth book in the Susan Wiles Schoolhouse mysteries. Diane also writes the Sugarbury Falls mysteries which she began recently. The first in that series is *A Deadly Course*.